ZOMBACON

an exquisite corpse style anthology

Edited by Robert Royal Poff

Zombacon

Paperback ISBN: 979-8-9861529-5-0

eBook ISBN: B0CW1JP54B

Edited and formatted by 360 Editing (a division of Uncomfortably Dark).

Editor: Candace Nola. Mort Stone.

Cover Art by Matt Wildasin

First Edition

Contents

Dedication

This book is dedicated to, and in part funded by, the incredible:

Paul Grammatico
Christian Warner
Joe Pesavento
Jess Unrein
Tasha Reynolds

Chapter One

by Matt Wildasin

"AND THAT DOES IT for the weather report. Next up on the show, we have a soft rock block of your favorite hits and—" The radio station blipped between audio and static before it fizzled out.

"Ah, shit..." Travis Sunderland slurred as he reached for the radio knob and fumbled through the stations.

It was midnight, and Travis was midway through hauling the ordered cargo from coast to coast. This time, he was pulling a tanker full of what he assumed to be a highly prized liquid, as the price for transporting it was astronomical. Though the job was deemed urgent, he decided to spend the first two days ordered for travel lounging about at home. In order to make up for the lost time, he knew he'd have to pull a few all-nighters. Besides playing some road games to occupy himself, the radio was his bastion for entertainment.

He continued to turn the dial, watching the orange needle from the corner of his eye scroll horizontally through the numbers. The dashboard gave off a faint green glow, bathing the inside of the cab in the luminescence. The truck was old and therefore did not have a TV mount, a mini fridge, or even a self-scanning radio. What the rig lacked in luxury it made up for in making him money. As a private contractor with a truck of his own, any money made over simple maintenance was cherry. In staying frugal with his truck, he could pocket the profit. Still, on nights like this, he wished he had at least sprung for a new radio.

After some time messing with the controls, Travis managed to find a clear channel. He rested the dial on the station and listened.

"If you're out there listenin', I want you to place your hand on your stereo and give yourself to Jesus!" an older sounding man hailed as a poorly played organ accompanied him.

"Sumabitch..." Travis said as he reluctantly dropped his hand and gave up. This would have to do for the time being—there was nothing else but static.

In the passenger seat next to him was a brown paper bag, the bottom drenched with grease. A logo of a smiling cartoon cow peeking through a bright yellow sun adorned the bag. The fast-food joint's name, 'Cow Patties,' was printed in red in an overly italic font that made it hard to read. Travis had never heard of this establishment, but he couldn't care less. They had a double bacon cheeseburger with a huge side of fries and a root beer float on the menu—his trifecta of junk food bliss. As far as he was concerned, they could have straight up called it Cow Shit Burgers and he still would have ordered there.

The burger smelled divine; the aroma of grilled beef, salty bacon, and grease wafted from the bag as he opened it and fished through its contents. He would save the burger for last, though, just to stretch the meal for as long as he could. Hauling a rig for a living led Travis to adopt a different lifestyle for eating, though not a health conscious one. Life on the road had very few options in the way of palatable beneficial items. He had to eat his meals in parts at a time, so he could keep one eye on the road while shoveling the sometimes-questionable foods he chose for sustenance into him.

As he rammed the first copious fistful of overly salted and partially wilted fries into his mouth, a warning cut in over the radio:

"This is News Eight bringing you this breaking story: a multi car pile-up has caused major backups on Route 30. Local officials reported three deaths. The road is closed to traffic temporarily until the accident can be cleared. Motorists are encouraged to find alternate routes. News Eight will now return you to your regularly scheduled programming."

The jingle for News Eight played briefly before the reverend returned to the station, claiming, "Those of you who have not taken the Lord into your home will face damnation in Hell! And those of gluttonous intent with bulbous bellies full of processed filth will—"

"Yeah, yeah, burn in Hell," Travis mumbled through another handful of fries. He thought about changing the station, but he was starving and chose instead to continue chowing down and swallow his righteous guilt.

One thing he did have to find, however, was an alternate route. The highway would have been a straight shot, but he couldn't risk losing more time. What he was hauling needed to be dropped off in a timely manner; they paid big, but they also penalized heavily, sometimes docking payment by the hours beyond estimated arrival. Travis held off on eating for a moment to program his GPS machine; an old Garmin he bought at a yard sale a few years back.

It was never updated, so it didn't have new roads coded in, but old back roads were still in the system. After a few moments of calculating, the GPS found a route that would take him through some old farmland. The chosen alternate would cost him an hour of extra travel, but he figured he could make that up by pissing in some jars and holding his bowels until absolutely necessary. His Ocean Cove dream was not going to get away.

Travis glanced over at a photo he had pinned to his sun visor. It was a greeting card from his last trip to Ocean Coast. He was planning to move there and retire at the upcoming ripe early age of fifty-five. This load was going to fund the down payment on his condominium.

The GPS indicated the next exit as his turnoff, and he obeyed. A sign along the off-ramp read: PIG PEN'S SWINE FARM. The subtitle beneath the name read: 'Come see our prize-winning pigs and pet them too!' He thought it weird that someone would make a petting zoo out of a sloppy, muddy pig farm, but then again, he was a guy from the suburbs; the small-town farm life was foreign to him. According to his GPS, Travis would be driving right by Pig Pen's farm. He didn't have time to stop, of course, but he was interested in seeing what a farm such as this would look like.

AFTER SOME TIME OF driving down dark serpentine roads, the clear night sky became overcast, then unleashed the rain in sheets. It was time for

Travis to devour his now cold bacon cheeseburger. He fished it out of the bag, carefully removed its wrapper, then sat it upon the dash. He was surprised to see how the burger still looked fresh, which made his mouth water in anticipation. Travis grabbed hold of the burger and sunk his teeth in for his first bite, then sat it back on the wrapper. The rain beat down as he savored the flavor. He licked his lips as a streak of lightning flashed behind a cluster of dark clouds. A storm like this would usually cause Travis to drive more carefully, but he felt starved and couldn't wait any longer to consume something, so he decided to multitask.

The winding roads finally gave way to a long, straight stretch. He eyed the delectable burger and swiped it up from the dash once again. He scarfed down several bites as he saw signs for Pig Pen's Swine Farm along the way, marking down the miles until arrival. He also saw signs for a city named Opossum Falls and a restaurant called The Old Stone Mill, labeled as 'Five-Star Dining set in the calming wilds of Old Town America.' It seemed odd to him for such a place to be out in the middle of nowhere, let alone in a town called Opossum Falls. Regardless of the unusual location choice, he would be passing through that town, so he hoped to catch a glimpse of the joint.

Travis took the last bite of his burger as he saw a tall sign for Pig Pen's in the distance: a long pole stretched for what seemed like miles into the night sky and shined like a massive yellow beacon over the darkened establishment. It was then that Travis' eyelids grew heavy, and he felt himself nodding off. The comforting taste of the burger that filled his stomach made him overly tired.

"No, no...we ain't doing this," he muttered aloud as he slapped his cheeks, desperately trying to ward off the oncoming food coma.

He kept his sights on Pig Pen's sign as he took slurps of the flat and soupy root beer float. He hoped the sugar would help, but it only seemed to exacerbate the issue. Travis fought the good fight against lack of sleep and consumption of slop, but as the reverend on the radio shouted, "Repent now! Your day of judgment is at hand!" Travis's eyes fluttered closed.

His truck careened off the road, crashing through the rickety fences surrounding Pig Pen's Swine Farm. The front of the rig collided with a sizable quartz boulder in the grazing field. The truck jackknifed and the tanker skid several feet before rolling and landing sideways.

The impact caused Travis to crack his head against the dash, fracturing his skull and tearing open his forehead. The gash in his skin spouted blood like a freshly popped champagne bottle. The tanker he was hauling, much like his head, had also broken open and oozed gallons of toxic green sludge into the small brook flowing through the field that lead back into the farm's water well.

The well-worn postcard for Ocean Cove still hung tightly on the visor in Travis' cab. The bright sunny shores amidst the card were the last thing he struggled to see before he bled out. Travis' death unknowingly changed the way people saw pigs forever.

The Luau

"GET THOSE DAMNED PIGS glazed and in the rotisserie! I'm not eighty-sixing the main course tonight!" Chef Mason Peters shouted over the bustling noise of his kitchen.

The Old Stone Mill was hosting a Hawaiian-themed celebration; something that Mason had planned and prepped for over a year. He even struck a deal with the local pig farm to supply them with pigs for the main dishes, which almost didn't happen after a freak truck accident involving a toxic spill a couple of weeks back nearly shut down the farm. Luckily, the pigs were deemed unharmed, so everything went on as scheduled.

"Yes, chef!" his team shouted in response as they frantically continued to prepare desserts and other dishes that would accompany the exceptionally large feast.

Mason planned a seven-course meal starting with an amuse-bouche consisting of a poké made with glazed pork belly and smoked salmon over rice balls. All the dishes would include pork in some fashion, leading up to the main dish of open pit pig roasts.

This was something that the town of Opossum Falls had never seen before. The word of it stretched far and wide, drawing in crowds from all over the area and neighboring cities. Mason cut his teeth in Las Vegas, so his reputation was well regarded and followed him to The Old Stone Mill that he opened in a sleepy small town and transformed it into one of the best restaurants in the Midwest. Tonight would be one of his masterpiece selections—nothing could go wrong.

Mason watched through the porthole window, through the double swinging doors that separated the kitchen from the dining room. He stroked his freshly shaven chin as he watched dinner guests file in and take their seats. The Mill was decorated with potted palm trees and hibiscus flowers. A performance of Maui war dances entertained guests as Mason and his team prepped the amuse bouche course.

"Chef, we have a small problem," his sous chef, Gloria Holmes, blurted out in a frantic flurry.

Mason turned to her and, in an annoyed tone, replied, "This better be good."

She fumbled over her words for a moment. Mason could see in her eyes that what was about to come out of her mouth was going to put a damper on the evening. Her hesitation irritated him. "Spit it out! What's wrong?"

"Flora, sir...she's in the bathroom complaining of stomach pain."

Mason breathed a sigh of relief and half laughed as he asked, "Is that all? Just someone has a tummy ache?"

"Well, it's...she was tasting the starter, so..."

Mason shook his head, choosing not to believe there was a correlation. "She has a problem with everything. I honestly don't know why she works in kitchens with such a sensitive stomach." He waved Gloria away and added, "It's fine. Just serve the food. And when Flora feels better, she can come back."

Gloria insisted, "But, sir...I really think you should see her. She doesn't look—"

Mason sighed loudly, interrupting her, then spat, "Fine!" He looked past Gloria to his kitchen staff that were frantically running about preparing food and instructed, "Keep cooking and don't miss a beat with those dishes!"

Mason and Gloria crept into the women's bathroom. They didn't want to shock Flora, so they kept quiet until they neared the stall she was in. Gloria spotted her kitchen clogs peeking out from just under the stall door.

"Flora, hun...Mason and I are here to check on ya. You, ok?"

A groan came from the stall, followed by a sound that no human should be able to make. It sounded like screeching, but more swine-like than human.

Mason and Gloria both stepped backward from the door at the sound, then Mason whispered, "What the fuck was that?"

Another squeal came from the stall as Flora's clogs shot across the room. A heavy blow hit the stall door, denting it. A clacking sound echoed through the room as two hoof-shaped appendages reached the tiled floor.

"F-Flora?" Gloria stammered out. She was so frightened that the word nearly stuck in her throat.

Another heavy slam against the door echoed through the bathroom as a hoofed foot smashed into it. The door broke at the hinges, soared from the stall, crashed into the hand sink across from it, and shattered the mirror above the sink. A light fixture by the mirror also broke from the wall; the bulb flickering from the strained wiring.

They watched as Flora emerged from the stall. Her body was mangled and mutated into a human-pig chimera. She stood upright, nearly nine to ten feet tall, with her jet-black hair sweeping over the floor. Her body was bulbous and covered with fine peach fuzz-like pink hair. Flora's nose had become misshapen; the cartilage had broken in on itself, making her nostrils flare and face frontward. She squealed and wailed in horror and agony as copious amounts of drool and vomit oozed from her mouth.

"What the fuck?!" Mason screamed as he ran from the bathroom.

"Hey wait!" Gloria yelled, but it was too late. Mason had run from the bathroom and locked it from the outside. Gloria's cries for help turned into screams of terror, then were drowned out by the gurgling of blood.

Mason sprinted back to the kitchen, planning to phone the police from his office as he prayed to God that the bathroom door would hold, but as he rounded the corner from the facilities, he stumbled upon the nightmare his kitchen had transformed into. What was left of his staff was being overrun by hordes of pig-like monsters. Some were covered in tattered chef jackets, while others wore the remains of suits and fine dresses. The kitchen was coated in blood and intestines, the walls were dripping with gore as human-like entrails were strewn about over shelves and pan hooks.

A chef's decapitated head bobbed in a pot of boiling Saimin. Shrill screams were nearly drowned out by the horrendous bellows of the creatures as they tore flesh and meat from the bones of his staff. Fires broke out as sauté pans overheated, causing the room to fill with smoke that set off the Ansul system, and a dense fog rained down, blanketing the dreadful scene.

Mason skulked through the mist to retreat to the dining room. As the swinging doors closed behind him, Mason found himself face-to-face with a packed room of pig-like abominations. What unfortunate souls were unmutated were stains upon the walls and carpet. The monstrous pigs set their blood-lusting sights upon him. Like a pack of feral wolves, the horde of swine raised their heads and squealed into the blood-soaked night. Mason felt their dull teeth rip him apart for only a few excruciating minutes before his head was finally cleaved from his body.

Chapter Two

by Robert Royal Poff

"LOOK, MAN, ALL I'M saying is it makes perfect sense. Our fucking eyes, man, they see everything, but they're not actually interpreting things as they are. Everything around us is just this... this weird hallucinatory series of chemical reactions that our brains use to make sense of the world around us. Nothing is real. Like color, it's just a collective opinion that dictates what we designated as color. There is no color blind, there are only brains that interpret differently."

"Shit, man, that's some heavy stuff." Alberto leaned forward, dipping the end of a blunt into a decorative ashtray designed to look like a screaming face. He smashed the end into the ashes, watching as the smoke flickered and died. "You're tripping pretty fucking hard right now, aren't you?"

Damien's legs kicked out, his body contorting so he could push his bearded face over the table, his glasses drooping slightly on his boxy face. "Think about it, man. Everything we've ever known is just a collection of what we've been told to be true. Shrooms, acid, the reason that shit fucks with our brains the way it does is because it's showing us a new path of perception. Take this fucking table," he rapped his knuckles on the table rhythmically, "I'm not actually touching shit. The molecules of my hand never make contact with the molecules that make up the table. Fact. There's an ocean of distance unperceivable to us, there's this... intermolecular space that's always present and yet I still feel. I still know what a table's hardness is like, despite never actually making contact.

It's absurd, right? That's because we're constantly hallucinating a world around us that doesn't actually exist because our brain chemistry has decided it to be so. Tell him, Burchell!"

He slapped the leg of a body stretched out adjacent to him, pulling the man from his stupor as his eyes withdrew from the ceiling. David kicked out his spider-like leg, his foot connecting with Damien's ribs. "The fuck, man?" Damien roared.

"Felt pretty damn real, didn't it?" David spat, chuckling a bit. His eyes were so squinted that the color barely leaked through leaden lids. "I hate your little solipsism rants. You take some shrooms and you're like the next fucking Aristotle, kinda look like him, too." He held up his hands like he was forming a TV screen with them, hoisting them up to Damien's face, who soured dramatically.

Adam laughed, peering through the room as a lingering trail of ghastly tendrils permeated the air. His eyes perused the table where a half-eaten fast food bacon cheeseburger lingered in its own grease filled basin, attracting the attention of a fly that greedily whizzed by. "Has anyone seen Michael?"

"He's probably off snorting something in the bathroom."

"I don't know why he hides that shit like we don't already know," Alberto scoffed. "I gotta piss." He stood, wandering off to the bathroom as the corners of his vision began creeping in with a blackened haze. He knocked on the door. No response. "You better not have pulled an Elvis in there or Damien's gonna be pissed." Still nothing. Alberto briefly considered barging in, but when he fiddled with the handle, the door was locked. He turned, his vision spinning past his body as the world crashed around him and he began his trek outside. The night consumed the house as he dropped his pants, clumsy hands reaching through the darkness, and he felt instant relief as he pissed onto the fencepost.

His eyes fluttered toward the bushes, his vision blinking in and out as the sounds of rustling consumed his thoughts. His eyes stopped dead, as something lurked within the shadows, two glowering moons constricting the air in a viselike grip. He stared; it stared back. He was about to call out when a crash erupted from inside the house, followed by a perilous scream. He shook, zipping his pants and ran inside.

Immediately upon entry, he felt the vibes of the room shift. The air stood deathly quiet, and the smoke had begun dissipating out the door, no longer fueled by the blunts they had been passing around. Alberto's legs shook as he fought off the urge to call out to his friends. He made it about halfway down the hall when more bellowing wails shook the house, consuming the air in a vapid otherworldliness akin to something straight out of a horror movie. He turned the corner, rearing his head around unsteadily, and saw the horrific scene unfold before him.

Blood. Blood littered the table, dripping onto a rapacious floor that lapped up the crimson puddle. Reality slurred as he followed the trail to a body. The caved in face was a mock visage of what his friend David had been mere moments before. The exposed muscles still twitched, sputtering blood onto the carpet as the rag-dolled corpse crashed its torn apart mouth in an empty, gaping scream, as if the jaw had been forcefully ripped from the rest of the face. Alberto's eyes lingered for as long as his mind could bear before flickering to any other detail. The imprint of the corpse still burned into his vision as more horrors took hold. Organs wrapped the room, looping in intricate patterns around the table and retreating behind the couch where they disappeared from view.

He motioned forward, but before he could take a step, a great beast rose from behind the couch, stuffing its face full of bloodied organs. It wore Michael's face, stretched across a bulbous frame, no longer shaped like anything even adjacent to a man. It towered, the rim of its deformed spine rubbing the ceiling as each bone nearly stabbed through the stretched-out layer of muscle tissue. Damien's whimpers struck the air as the beast snorted, its great body heaving dramatically as blood and bile fell from daft lips. Skin pulled across grooves and bones like the skin of a child, struggling to mold to its host.

"What... the... fu-"

"-KING HELL, MAN, THAT'S so good." Alberto dropped the burrito onto his plate, licking the splattering of grease and leftover chunks of sauce off his fingers. "Absolutely incredible, as always." He spun the plate around so the camera recording him could pick up the sizable bite mark. "A solid nine out of ten, what can I say? Burrito House doesn't disappoint. Truly, everything off their menu is as close to perfect as I've seen. Well, this has been Alberto, signing off." He scrubbed the grease onto his shirt before flipping the switch on the camera and watching the little red light die.

Immediately he felt his body relax, the muscles that always tensed during filming eroding into a calmed state. He spun the camera around, readying himself to check the footage, when a buzzing electrocuted the room, sending his limbs into a spiral of erratic gestures. He hadn't always been like this, but the accident had left him changed, something he hadn't been before that invaded his consciousness with torturous thoughts of an ever-increasing intensity. He let his heart settle for a second, clutching his beating chest as the ringing smacked down silence like a kid with a bat. He moved toward the intercom by the door, checking as the ringer sounded off in chimes. A firm layer of dust piled up from its misuse. "H-hello?" His voice was gruff, off-putting even to himself as annoyance gargled up from his throat.

"Well, are you gonna let me in or what?" the box responded.

"Who is this?"

"Who's the only person to ever visit your stupid ass? Hurry up and let me in."

He unlocked the door, and it was mere seconds later that a foreign invader had intruded upon his sanctum. Reby didn't stop to acknowledge him, pushing past and began fiddling with the TV. "You're not gonna fucking believe this."

"Hello, Reby, and welcome to my house. Make yourself at home," he scoffed.

She waved him off. The TV flickered to life, showcasing multiple rows of colored stripes with the text "PLEASE STAND BY" plastered over the top.

"What the-"

"It's on every channel," she cut him off, flipping through each channel to add validity to her claim. "Every fucking one, except one."

The TV blared to life, sounding off as the image of a news reporter flickered in its frame, teetering in and out of sparse nothingness. "-locals within a ten-mile radius are being advised to stay within their homes and make no further contact with those outside. Do not, under any circumstances, open your doors for anyone, stranger or otherwise, and call the police if the need for assistance arrives-"

"Look, look, are you seeing this?" Reby prodded at the TV with a shaking finger, her head pivoting constantly from Alberto to the announcer.

"Yeah, they're saying don't leave your house."

"Yeah!"

"So why the fuck are you here?"

She shrugged. "When have I ever listened to what I'm told? Now, shh. Watch!"

Alberto's mouth dropped to argue, his scarred face wrinkling awkwardly around skewed lips, when the news reporter morphed into a cityscape. His city. The vantage point of the footage as well as the grainy texture would suggest it came from a security cam. He watched as the street below piled with a clusterfuck of bodies that held all the renaissance grandeur and chaotic movement of a powerful piece of art. Great waves of people scattered in all directions as what appeared to be grotesque, deformed humanoid mounds interspersed the crowd, tackling various people to the ground where they didn't rise.

Gunfire lit the air, dropping anything it touched indiscriminately. He found his body slowly inching towards the screen, eyes dancing around to make out any of the creatures in the jumble of movement, but everything was too fast. He watched as one of the great beasts tackled a woman to the ground, tearing at her with greedy hands that yanked something akin to a wet snake from her side before shoveling it towards a bulbous, deformed mouth.

He once again went to speak when a curt crash of broken glass permeated from somewhere just past his apartment's door. Then the screaming came. A woman, his neighbor Darlene, squealed before her voice ended just as suddenly as it had begun, like her vocal cords had snapped from the stress. For a while, there was nothing. Then more breaking glass, followed by more screaming. This time it was closer, maybe three rooms down. He turned towards Reby, who was already on her feet. She slid to the balcony, peaking over the ledge and Alberto somehow knew what she was going to say before she said it. "Come on, we can get out through here."

"You wanna jump that? This is the fourth fucking floor. Why not break my legs now in the comfort of my home?"

"We don't need to jump all the way. Just repel ourselves down to the floor below. Wash, rinse, repeat." She hefted her legs over the railing gracefully, pirouetting her body in subtle twists as her loose clothes swished with the breeze. She gave a salute before dropping and disappearing from sight.

Alberto cocked his head to the side, awaiting the splatter that never came. Instead, her voice rang out, "See? Easy as that."

He walked over, inspecting her as she stood, hands on hips, defiance in her eyes as she stared back at him. Something heavy crashed into the door, attempting to get in. Someone was attempting to get in. Alberto made one last look at his home, a haven he hadn't purposefully abandoned in months, and was forced to leave the details to memory as he let his body drop. They repelled like mountain climbers, Reby much more experienced at acts of parkour from her rich history of running from police during protests. The second their feet touched the ground, they were met by chaos as hordes of bodies flung themselves in every direction, some clambering inside houses while others pushed their way out into the streets.

Reby grabbed for his hand, the first physical interaction he had since the incident, and began dragging him down the street just as a crashing car spiraled through some bodies and into a lamppost where great plumes of smoke billowed out of its crashed in hood. The driver crawled out of the wreckage and was quickly trampled by the crowd, his screams lost in the cacophony of sound as Reby and Alberto ran.

They dodged, weaving in and out of clusters as they took off. "Where are we going?" Alberto wailed.

"Away. Far away."

They turned a corner and were met by dozens of bodies sprinkling the ground, half of which had great beasts leaning over them, feasting on flesh, muscle, and bone indiscriminately. They snorted and squealed, occasionally hefting great hog-like heads into the air to throw back chunks of meat into their blood smeared mouths. Each bore human eyes, wide from an agonizing pain Alberto knew far too well. Reby went to stifle a scream, but the nearest boar heard them, prodding a sniffling snout in their direction as some mismatched tusks bruxed against the skin, poking holes through layers of flesh and nearly curling back into the face.

It stood clumsily on two legs of different lengths; the bones twisted to bend like that of a swine's, completely disregarding the humanoid stance as it began to gallop towards them. They ran back into the busy streets, tearing past beast and man alike as they scrambled for any spot that'd be safe. They took shelter in an alleyway, bouncing in boundless strides, turning behind a building. Reby's rapid turnovers lead the charge but dug into the ground to slow her pace as they realized they had hit a dead end. Behind them, the thunderous clap of hooves proved the beast still gave chase, its breathing coming in uneven wails. They turned, steeling themselves for their fate as the great hog took the bend carelessly, denting the brick wall as it crashed into it and immediately began its charge once more.

Alberto cowered, nearly feeling the beast's warm, metallic scented breath upon his neck when its head suddenly exploded. Its eyes burst from the skull, fluttering like flower petals as its snout splintered into a million blood-soaked pieces, chunks of tongue and muscle structure raining down on Alberto's face, flooding the folds of his eyes as they widened. Its body lumbered forward another few steps, the momentum keeping it going, so Alberto and Reby had to jump out of the way as its hulking frame crashed to the ground, sliding a few feet on its own bloodied stump.

Alberto's eyes whipped around wildly as a voice called past the blood that dripped over his vision, "Well, I'll be. That was a little too close for comfort." He locked sight on a woman as she held open a door they must've missed, beckoning them over. She was plump, maybe 5'1 with a honey-comb hairstyle that swished around some upturned bangs like half a can of hairspray had gone into keeping each strand at just the right shape.

Her thick, blushed cheeks curled into pursed lips, but she hefted a shotgun with such familiarity that she looked almost soldier-like despite her design. "Well, come on then. I'da be runnin' all over hell's half acre if I were you kids," she cawed in a thick southern accent. "Trumpet like that's just gonna attract more of 'em."

Chapter Three

by Nathan D. Ludwig

For the love of Jesus, Harold, take me to wherever you are right now. I can't stand it anymore down here.

Bertha McFadden prayed to her late husband, Harold McFadden, as she watched the depressing news cycle repeat itself on Vox News. She had lost the remote to her pre-smart 40-inch flat screen television shortly after Harold passed and couldn't scare up enough effort to conduct a proper search for it. Her damned hip wouldn't allow such nonsense.

Between the vague insinuations that the current president was both a pedophile and a communist, and subject matter experts claiming the Democratic Party had a moon base full of child slaves and delicious pizza, Bertha could hardly catch her breath. The world was going straight to Hell in a socialist handbasket, and she felt like there wasn't a damn thing she could do about it.

Her seventy-nine years on this planet put her face-to-face with a lot of unbearable hardships. Her parents divorcing. Her mother committing suicide. Her father drinking himself to death. Harold being unable to have kids. A murderer's row of trials and tribulations. Through it all, she relied on her close relationship with God and Jesus himself to see her through it all. But *this* - watching her beloved country get torn to shreds by these gay hipsters and milzennial teeny boppers - was a bridge too far from her humble point of view. Harold would be rolling in his urn if he could see the parade of decadence and orgiastic lack of self-control that Vox News expertly exposed on a daily basis. The news was never his favorite show, but he'd sit up and take notice of all this; she was sure of it.

Bertha checked her phone again. Clicked on an app that said "Bam-Cart". Colorful, blocky letters over the image of a shopping cart with a rocket attached to it. She swiped over to the status of her order.

"Your order is taking longer than expected. We will notify you when a BamCart professional has begun filling your order."

Good for nothing, piece of junk. I want my groceries yesterday!

She refused to go shopping on her own anymore. Not with all those ungodly heathens out there, trying to turn everyone into androgynous criminals. Breeding with each other until everyone was one color of dull brown or something like that. That's what her favorite commentator on Vox said the other night. Rand Guggenheim. He was handsome. And so knowledgeable. Her nephew, Craig, said Rand was a fascist. Like that little shit even knew what an actual fascist was. *He* didn't fight the Nazis back then. Her Harold didn't, either. But the point was, they were at least alive for the end of the war. And that counted for something, she believed. Born into patriotism, whether anyone liked it or not!

Craig also offered to go shopping for her once a week. That was a sweet gesture from such a heathen relative. His gaged ears made her gag whenever she saw them. And that was on top of the stench of marijuana that seemed to follow him everywhere he went. Her doctor recommended she take some to ease her arthritis, but there was no way that quack from India or wherever was going to get her hooked on reefer. She wasn't about to go on welfare anytime soon if she could help it. Craig got tired of being called on the carpet for forgetting her Mallomars and wine coolers, saying something about them not being good for her. Who the hell did he think he was?

After a sound browbeating a few weeks ago, he set up a few apps on her phone and never came back to even visit. An app for takeout delivery called SmashFood. It came in handy for ordering Chinese and Mexican, her favorites by far. An app for a taxi service that seemingly operated out of random people's houses named CarGo, for when she needed a ride to church. And of course, BamCart. The bane of her existence.

She eyeballed the areas of her apartment that she could see as she fumed. Not much had changed since Harold had left her three years ago. It was smallish, but it was home and there wasn't anything on God's green earth that could take her away from the comfort and solitude the place provided her. Her social security more than paid for the rent and left just enough each month for food, the occasional trip to the horse track for a Saturday of slots and hard sodas, and the occasional online purchase. Considering the circumstances, life was good. Praise Jesus.

She wasn't much of a cleaner anymore, but she stayed on top of it best she could. It was only her now, anyways. A little laundry here, a few dishes there. Nothing some Febreze and a few pushes of a Swiffer couldn't fix. Craig sure as hell wasn't going to come over and do it. Young people just didn't want to work anymore, she was certain, and that kid was living proof.

Most of the apartment smelled like mothballs and orange juice, and she liked it that way. As she gazed longingly onto her "Wall of Fame," tears welled up in her eyes at the sight of Harold's last Sears studio portrait hanging next to framed photos of Ronald Reagan, George W. Bush, and Donald Trump. Her framed photo of Richard Nixon had broken when Harold had fallen against it, keeled over, and dropped dead. "He took Nixon with him," she liked to tell people, thinking they would find it as funnily bittersweet as she did. Most didn't. But what did they know? Harold looked so good in his plaid sweater vest and maroon alligator polo shirt. No hair, no real teeth, but the same man she married almost sixty years ago.

As she wiped a few tears from her astigmatism-addled eyes and took her bifocals off her petite head and gave them a wipe with her salmon cardigan, a thumping, bumping commotion came from the apartment upstairs. The commie Hispanics that moved in a few months ago. They were usually quiet. Never introduced themselves. Sometimes she could hear salsa or merengue music coming from up there, but hardly ever an honest-to-God commotion like this. It sounded like a pro-wrestling match was going on up there, like the shows Harold loved to watch when he was among the living. She hated them outright and thought they were stupid, but they made him happy, so she allowed the idiocy to emanate from their TV until he fell asleep in his dumpy recliner across from the couch - her haven. And once he was asleep, it was back to Vox News.

"Quiet up there! I'm trying to watch the—"

A final, deafening THUD came from "up there" and then nothing. Sounded like someone died. Or all of them at once. It gave her a slight case of the heebie-jeebies.

"...news."

No sooner than she could finish her interrupted thought out loud, a special report shoved its way over the regularly scheduled truth-telling on Bertha's news channel of choice.

A grim, hangdog-faced anchor, one of the ones she thought might be a closet liberal sympathizer, began speaking in a hushed, reserved tone. A look of inescapable worry right there for everyone to see. Her long blonde hair, deep blue eyes, and generic good looks were rendered utterly useless as footage of something Bertha couldn't even decipher appeared in a window next to the anchor. The anchor's name was right there on a chyron at the bottom of the screen, but what Bertha saw on the footage made her forget everything about the anchor. Especially her name.

"This is a Vox News Special Report....

"What in God's name—"

"... We are getting word from several major cities all over the world that a mysterious virus is spreading like wildfire, seemingly infecting people with a form of swine flu that apparently transforms the recipient into a massive, feral, mutant pig-like creature with extremely violent and bloodthirsty tendencies."

The anchor paused for a moment, an obvious hitch in her voice. She couldn't seem to believe the footage, either. Alternating clips played of chaos and mayhem on various major city streets. People ran wildly for their lives, chased by monstrous pig-like people. Some kept running. Others were devoured right there live on camera, their bodies ripped apart by teeth, tusks, trotters, and misshapen hand-claws that dug into flesh like jagged shovels of hard chitin. It would have made Bertha violently ill if it weren't so mind-numbingly fascinating. Some of the fleeing populace transformed into the same pig people they were being chased by right before her eyes. Her jaw hung open as the new pig people mated with the original pig people in an orgy of blood, semen, urine, and feces.

And *that* made her vomit. All over her lap and the couch and the floor. There went her microwave pot stickers and Diet Coke she had for lunch. *What a waste of five bucks*, she thought involuntarily.

"The CDC and the World Health Organization are urging people not to travel and to stay indoors and lock themselves inside as securely as possible. There is currently no known source, cause, cure, or reason for the virus yet. All major government organizations are recommending that people not eat any meat products, especially, and we must stress this, especially pork products. There could be a possible link to eating pork and turning into a ravenous porcine mutant. We will have more information as soon as it's available. In the meantime, we will stay with this startling and bracing footage that is being provided to us by brave videographers all over the globe."

As if it was even possible, the carnage and coitus on her screen got even more heinous and feverish, to the point where it was extremely difficult to even make out exactly what was going on anymore. Horrific pig monsters filled the streets in each shot, with less and less of anything resembling a normal human being remaining that hadn't either been completely eviscerated or violated in some way, shape or form.

It's the end times... Dear God...

"Glory, glory hallelujah! The end times are upon us! The Lord has deemed it necessary to rid the world of the sinners and the swine infecting our world. Apparently literally!"

As she celebrated, Bertha almost slipped on her own puke. She sat back down just as quickly as she stood up. Broken hip averted. This time.

She checked her BamCart app again.

"We are experiencing uncommonly long wait times. Please be patient and a certified BamCart delivery technician will be in touch with you as soon as possible with your order."

Damn fangled technology. I could use a blessed wine cooler right about now.

It was time to get changed and get ready to embrace the apocalypse. Those disgusting pig things weren't going to get a leg up on her, no sir. When an opportunity presented itself, Bertha Rosaline McFadden answered the call.

And then the door to her apartment exploded inward. It fell to the ground in a deafening SLAM and a body flew through the air and landed on the floor right in front of her television. Just feet away from her. In the split second that followed, she instantly recognized who it was.

Jimmy Lindo. The Black kid from across the hall. She thought he was either fifteen or sixteen. He was nice enough to introduce himself when he and his family moved in a few years ago. Harold liked them, but she had a bad feeling about them. Especially him. She couldn't put a finger on it, but it was there.

"You broke my door, young man. How are you going to pay for—?"

Seemingly summoned by her annoyed voice, a massive, still-transforming pig thing lumbered through her doorway. It sort of looked like Sally Michaelson from a few doors down. Single parent. Kind of a loose woman if Bertha's opinion if the subject even mattered anymore. Her face contorted in a fat curl of pain as her nose pushed up and out, a trickle of blood snaking its way out of one of her nostrils. Most of her clothes were already ripped and torn at all the possible seams and a rank stench of shit wafted from her general frame. It was a horrible sight to witness in person, and it made Bertha want to pray. Not for Sally, but for herself. Just being near this kind of Satanic happening made her wish she'd kept her rosary on her at all times.

"Ms. McFadden, you gotta—"

"It's *Mrs.* McFadden, Jimmy. Just because my Harold is gone doesn't mean I'm back on the market all of a sudden. Don't you get any ideas."

The contorting, shifting piggy monster Bertha was sure used to be Sally took one stride over to Jimmy and lifted him up in the air, his head banging against the slap brush finish on her ceiling.

No, not the ceiling. What blasted app will I need to get that *fixed?*

"*Mrs.* McFadden, please—"

Jimmy looked scared out of his mind, close to tears. It was too much to take in all at once. Who knew what this kid was up to on his own time out there? Up to no good, most likely. But he seemed so nice. Genuine, even. Regardless of whether he was about to die in her living room or not, he seemed nice.

"In the name of our lord Jesus Christ, I command you to unhand that boy!"

The Sally pig creature seemingly no longer spoke or understood English, because instead of responding or obeying, it simply opened its gaping, snaggle-toothed wild boar maw and brought Jimmy's head right toward it. A shrill, meaty, deep-throated squeal of hunger rushed forth from its diaphragm. The stench of rotting meat and putrid stomach acid followed right behind. It was so strong and pungent, it filled Bertha's apartment like rushing water into a sinking ship.

It's time, Harold. You were right.

Bertha reached deep into the seat cushion on her right (she preferred sitting in the middle, even when Harold was alive) and pulled out a Smith & Wesson .38 snub-nosed revolver (an anniversary gift the last year before Harold left the building, so to speak) and aimed hastily before yanking the trigger three times.

BLAM. BLAM. BLAM.

Three quick shots punched right into Piggy Sally's head, exploding chunks of flesh, skull, and brain matter all over Bertha's walls, the floor, Jimmy, and on herself. *It was fine*, she thought. It blended with the fresh lunch vomit surprisingly well.

The quickly dying pig monster dropped Jimmy to the floor and took a few jangly steps backward with its clomping, misshapen trotters before falling to the floor in a foul-smelling heap of steaming hot pig flesh and the hair of a once human being interspersed throughout the jumble of grossness. The closest thing Bertha could relate it to was a cross between that pig roast luau she and Harold went to in Maui on their twenty-fifth anniversary crossed with the men's latrines at the VFW lodge in Reseda. Harold's Vietnam buddies were a disgusting bunch. This was pretty close to that.

Catching his breath and rubbing his neck, Jimmy looked up at Bertha and nodded in profuse thanks.

"Thank... Thank you... I thought I was a—"

"Rutting, Godless pig demon?"

"Goner was what I was gonna say. A goner, for real. On god, Mrs. McFadden."

"My door. You going to fix it?"

"...Seriously?"

"You're trespassing right now, technically."

"Have you... Have you even seen the news?"

"Yes. You interrupted me doing just that."

"So, then you know what's happening."

"The end times, boy. A strange way to happen, for sure, but the end times nonetheless."

Jimmy looked at her askance, seemingly unable to continue speaking. He must be tired. Maybe injured. That's probably it, yes.

"Look. There's a group of us in the complex that are trying to evacuate together. You know, strength in numbers. Some of us have weapons, others have supplies. Food. Water. But we gotta go now."

A flock? A herd to tend to? This is it. This is my calling. So be it.

"And you were coming to warn me, right? To make sure I was a part of this group, yes?"

"Well, I—"

"Say no more! I just need to clean this filth off of me and reload. You wait right here."

Praise the lord, Harold! It's time for us to serve our true purpose.

She tottered over to the mantel, just below her wall-mounted TV and gently grabbed a simple gray marble urn with a pewter lid. Harold's final resting place. She handed it gingerly to Jimmy, who held it to his chest with a confused look on his face.

"You hold on to Harold, and I'll grab the ammunition. Don't you move a muscle."

She made a mental note to grab her rosary, too. It was going to come in handy just as much as the gun, she surmised.

A lot of heathens out there. And they need saving. One way or the other.

Chapter Four

by Jessica Eppley

The Romp was particularly slow for a Friday night. There were a few of the regulars, yeah, but overall, the club was serving crickets. Sapphire Black finished out her new routine with only a handful of twenties in her gray lace G-string, and fuck, a few singles, too. She grabbed the wad of sweaty, crumpled bills and stuffed them into her rhinestone bra as she grumpily climbed off stage, her eight-inch stiletto heels clacking like the hooves of a pissed off horse.

With the blinding silvery lights obstructing her view, she wasn't able to make out the features of the heavyset man in the corner booth, but Sapphire already pegged him as a red flag from the moment he'd sat down. He wasn't drinking anything; he was alone, and he hadn't fished for his wallet once since she'd first gotten on stage to the club mix of AWOLNATION's *Sail* four minutes ago.

Sapphire Black, a.k.a. Genevieve LaRoe was a veteran dancer at The Romp. She'd worked here back when it was called Down Bad, before the renovations and the new owner classed up the place, upgrading it from a seedy strip club at the edge of town to a seedy strip club at the edge of town with new DJ equipment and a slightly less cockroach infested kitchen.

Her long, wavy hair, falling to her waist in rivulets of raven black silk, high glass-cutter cheekbones, and large bedroom eyes of cerulean blue had helped her come up with her stage name. A sheen of sweat glistened on her deeply tanned skin, and Sapphire sashayed backstage to the dressing room. A quick peek at her phone told her that was all folks. It was nearly 3 AM, and her shift was over.

"Hey, Gen?"

It was the manager, Maxine, a fifty-ish woman with dark blonde hair and a thick figure. She was poking her head into the dressing room. "You got time for a Red Room request?"

"Fuck, yeah," Genevieve replied, almost too enthusiastically. "I'm fucking dying tonight."

"It's been slow for all of us," another stripper called Frita offered from her post in front of the makeup mirror. "Go get 'em, Sport."

"Make that money!" Velvet's high titter followed as Genevieve toweled off and headed right back out again, those stiletto heels punctuating every purposeful step.

She followed Maxine out into the bar again and shielded her eyes against the blinding lights, following the gaze of her manager to the corner booth. Great. The weirdo newbie. Boundaries were going to be crossed for sure.

"Take good care of him," Maxine whispered. "He paid double for you."

"For me?" Genevieve, now rolling as Sapphire, queried. "I've never even seen him in here before."

Maxine shrugged with one shoulder. "It's not our job to know his reasons, just to get his money. Go to it."

The older woman turned on her heel and left the nearly empty showroom. Sapphire locked eyes with the man in the booth as he stood, his gut catching on the table's end as he did so. Sapphire forced a flirtatious smile and shimmied up to him, taking his arm.

"Follow me, handsome," she purred, and led him towards the Red Room. "What's your name?"

The man cleared a wad of phlegm grossly from his throat before he answered in a timid wheeze, "Mike."

Sapphire tensed up at the sound of his voice. He sounded sick. She hoped he wouldn't pass it along to her. After an already slim week, she couldn't afford to miss work, and no one wanted to watch a stripper pause between dances to blow her nose.

"Take a seat, big boy."

The man sank heavily onto the red leather couch, his bulk causing the air to slowly whoosh from the cushions as he sank down into it. The Weeknd started crackling through the speakers. Sapphire began to shimmy side to side, running her manicured fingers down the curves of her breasts, over her exposed and pierced belly button, across her hips and thighs, all the while keeping her blue eyes on Mike. She smiled seductively at him even when he uncomfortably rummaged around in his pocket, clearly jerking off. It wasn't the first time, it certainly wouldn't be the last. And though unorthodox, her drive for extra cash made her hope he wouldn't jizz in his pants before she'd even had a chance to get through one song. The longer she could tease them, the bigger the tips would be.

"Tell me, Mike," Sapphire said huskily as she inched closer to him, rubbing her tits as she slung a dangerously pointy heel onto the section of booth beside him, giving him a good look at her long legs. "Where are you from?"

"Uh, Dallas," the man said nervously. Sapphire caught a whiff of his body odor as she climbed over him like a dismissive cat, shoving her breasts into his face. She wrinkled her nose, but only for a second, not wanting to put him off.

As she'd expected, the newcomer started to get a little more brazen as Sapphire upped the ante with her strip tease and flung her bra to the floor. The bulge in his pants became more noticeable. His hand left his pocket just long enough to reach forward to caress one of her breasts. Sapphire Black gave his hand a gentle slap.

"Touching is extra," she warned.

"I paid double," Mike balked, frowning.

"That's your problem, not mine."

Mike frowned again, and slipped a hand into his other pocket, pulling out a stiff handful of twenties. Sapphire batted her eyes at him as she daintily plucked the bills from his hand and shoved them into her waistband.

"That's a good boy," she crooned, and then without warning, seized Mike by his hair, and shoved his face between her breasts. He tensed at first, then gave a muffled moan of ecstasy.

"You here on business?" Sapphire asked casually while she let him motorboat her.

Mike came up for air long enough to hiss, "At the lab."

"The lab? You're a scientist?"

Sapphire slid up against him, laughing haughtily as she felt the sporadic jerking motion from the bulge at his crotch, and then the following wetness that could only mean he'd come in his pants.

"Dallas, huh?" she continued, not wanting to encourage an early end to her private show. Depending on his stamina, she could probably encourage that wet spot to grow bigger, as well as the wad of cash in her G-string.

Mike gave a raspy groan from the depths of her cleavage, and suddenly Genevieve LaRoe came back full force as she felt a stab of pinching pain in her right breast. She jumped back, screeching as fresh blood began to roll down her bare belly.

"Did you just fucking bite me?" Gen demanded, her hand to her chest. She scowled angrily at the customer, and then her face fell as she noticed all the color...ALL of it, had completely drained from Mike's flesh.

The ruddy, feverish tone he had come in with was stark white, though sweat poured from him like he'd just spent a day in the sauna. Then, the smell hit her, unmistakably shit. Mike stood quickly, and fresh diarrhea ran down his pant legs onto the seat behind him. Genevieve gagged and covered her mouth. Jesus, this guy was sicker than she'd suspected. She'd seen some fucked up things in her last four years as a stripper, but this was the first time someone had actually crapped themselves in the middle of a lap dance.

Suddenly, Mike doubled over and gurgled as he exploded from the other end, spraying bloody vomit all over the carpet. Genevieve cried out and ran for the closed door, banging on it to get someone's attention over the beat of the music.

"Get me outta here!" She called. "Maxine?"

A horrendous choking sound caused Genevieve to spin back around. Mike had gone to his knees into his own mess. His hands clutched at his face as blood erupted from his orifices. Then he howled in agony as something black and fleshy dangled out of his mouth like a dead eel. It was his tongue. Gen screamed again and threw herself at the door, realizing with dismay that it was blocked from the outside. Someone had shut her in with this diseased freak.

Mike groaned, and this time the sound was less human than it was animal-like. With a wet rip, he reached up and yanked the blackened tongue straight out of his mouth, flinging it aside. More black blood oozed from his mouth, and then Genevieve noticed that his fingers were fusing together and darkening, hardening, almost like...hooves?

He roared and rose to his feet, tearing the clothing from his body. His skin rippled and twisted as he did so, ripping open at the shoulders as a lump of bone matter protruded from his back. He vomited again, projecting it across the room and splashing Genevieve before she could leap out of the way. She could see that several of his teeth had come with it, and gagged, scrambling away on her backside. She reached down and pulled off one of her stiletto heels, preparing to fight him off if she had to. He was coming for her, his voice a phlegmy squeal, his skin sallow, his face a melting nightmare. Long jagged tusks burst from the sides of his cheeks, tearing his mouth into a ragged joker grin. He lumbered over her with hands that were now black misshapen hooves. Drool dripped copiously from his ruined mouth. The stench was overpowering.

"You fucking PIG!" Genevieve screamed as she swung her heel straight into the side of the Not-Mike thing gurgling over her. She felt the end plunge into weakened skull and burst through into gooey mush. It stuck there as the creature quailed in pain and clutched with its hoof-like paws at the heel embedded in its skull.

Gen jumped to her feet, covered in splatters of blood, drool, and vomit as she rammed her shoulder into the door with all her might, cheering when she felt it give a little. There was a body propped up against the door. It was what was left of Maxine. Her face was just gone, mangled to the point that it resembled hamburger meat. Gallons of blood must have covered the woman.

"Maxine!" she cried, but she had no time to bend down and check on the obviously dead strip club manager. The Not-Mike thing behind her had wrenched the shoe from its head, and was now barreling toward her, snarling.

With a mighty heave, Gen shoved the door all the way open, toppling Maxine's body over. And that's when she got a good look at the pandemonium overwhelming The Romp.

The floor, walls, tables and stage were all splattered in blood. Customers and staff alike were screaming as they tried to fend off more malformed monstrosities resembling Mike in one way or another. Frita was crawling across the blood slicked stage, clutching at the remains of her right leg. One of the things was gnashing and scrambling toward her, unable to hike its bloated form up onto the stage to finish her off. Genevieve watched in horror as the exposed muscle and tendon in her co-worker's leg started to blacken before her eyes. The woman's wails were cut off only by the gush of bloody vomit spurting from her mouth, and her skin began to ripple.

"Jesus Christ!" Genevieve shrieked, "She's turning into one of them!"

The floor dropped out of her stomach as Genevieve touched the bite wound on her bare breast. Was this about to happen to her? How fast did this disease take over? No time to worry about that now. One of the things, one that looked like it used to be velvet based on the tattered remains of the sequin romper clinging to the boil-infested, twisted flesh, was half-running, half-stumbling towards her. Its left leg was a mound of blue-black tumors spiraling down from shreds of what was once a toned thigh. It reached for her with spindly arms that were too long, and fingers that were fused together, but sprouted long dangerous looking curved black claws. Her face, if you could even call it a face anymore, had eyes sunken so far back into the malformed skull they almost weren't there. One ear hung on shreds of gristle from the side of her head. It threw its head back and squealed like a demented pig as it came for her.

Genevieve had to think fast. She lifted her foot and kicked at it with her remaining stiletto, and the heel drove into the protruding roll of sickly white flesh that was the Velvet pig beast's belly. She pulled back and found that her foot was now stuck in its flesh. The Velvet pig snorted in a manner that sounded almost like laughter. It seized her leg in one of its horrendous claws, sinking the razor ends into her calf. Genevieve screamed as she wrenched her leg back as hard as she could. Her foot came free of the shoe, and the claws raked down her skin as she pulled out of its grasp. The stiletto remained embedded in its stomach, looking like an oversized belly ring.

The nearly naked Genevieve spun on her heel and began to run for the door to the club, the screams and garbled wet splattering sounds thundering in her ears. Two of the piggish monstrosities were fighting over a corpse blocking the front door. One of them had the remains of the poor sap's feet in its hideous protruding maw and was shaking its head like a dog with a squeak toy. The other had the man's throat between its jaws, and its massive blocky head lowered. Three deformed tusks jutted from one side of its torn mouth. Its wrinkled, runny snout oozed green mucus as it snorted its displeasure back at the other. The two growled and snarled through their visceral tug-of-war match until, finally, the corpse's head separated from its neck in a flood of gore and blood. The first beast roared in triumph as it dragged the bulk of its kill backwards, leaving a small opening by the door. Gen decided to risk it.

She bolted for the door and seized the bloody handle, twisting it hurriedly as the loser of the tug-of-war match screeched and flung the head at her. She felt it bounce sickeningly off her back as she flung the door open and burst into the cold night air in nothing but a pair of lace panties.

The streets were alight with frantic headlights as cars screeched out of control amongst the lumbering pig monsters clamoring toward them. An SUV headed right toward one of the monsters, and the beast lowered its head like a bull and charged at it, connecting with the front end. Metal and glass exploded around it, and the right headlight went out as the creature's tusk went right through it. The horn blared angrily, but the pig monster had not been harmed, and was now clamoring over the hood and smashing through the windshield with one gnarled rock of a hand. Genevieve heard the driver's screams cut off suddenly when the deformed maw closed over his head, and then there was another crunch, and she looked away, eyes squeezed shut.

"Hey! Over here!"

The voice snapped her to attention. Genevieve opened her eyes and spun around, seeing what looked like a beat up version of the Mystery Machine rolling up over the curb. The window was rolled down, and a young man with a scraggly goatee and a blood streaked Hawaiian shirt was waving to her. Without thinking, Genevieve bolted down the street toward it, not caring who this guy was or what his intentions were. He was human; he was alive, and he was her only chance.

As she got closer, the streetlights illuminated the faded gray paint job and sliding side door that was already opening for her. A woman waved to her from the back.

"Hurry!"

Genevieve didn't have to be told twice. She reached for the woman's outstretched hand and leaped inside, and before her bare feet even connected with the van's metal floor, the driver stepped on it, and they careened off the curb, slamming into another piggish monstrosity as it did. The thing shrieked and went down head first, its ass end pointed to the moon, a remnant of backbone curling out of its hindquarters in a bloody ringlet of a tail.

The woman and Genevieve worked together to slide the door shut again as the driver maneuvered them through the nightmare. The neon sign of The Romp became smaller and smaller as they sped down the blood streaked road.

"I'm Reby," the woman finally said, sticking out a slender hand for Gen to shake. She nodded towards the driver. "That's Alberto. And in the passenger seat is Paula."

"What the fuck is going on?" Genevieve demanded, ignoring the hand.

"The end of the world, sweetheart," Alberto called from the front. "Welcome to the resistance."

"First," Reby added, "We're getting the fuck out of here."

Chapter Five

by Rowland Bercy, Jr.

"Boy, now don't you go dropping my dear sweet Harold," Mrs. McFadden called as she clamored around the bedroom. She retrieved her rosary and additional ammunition from the nightstand next to her bed. She draped the prayer bead around her neck and stuffed the bullets into her oversized pocketbook. Her knees popped with every step as she wandered from the bedroom into the living room to discover Jimmy rifling through her personal belongings.

"And just what do you think you're doing, young man?" she asked, standing in the doorway with an accusing hand on her hip. "You people never cease to amaze me. You have the gall to steal from me after I done rescued you from the clutches of the Prince of Darkness himself. You should be ashamed of yourself."

"Umm... I... I wasn't stealing nothing," Jimmy stammered in reply. "I was just looking for a weapon to defend myself."

Mrs. McFadden relaxed and smiled. "Well, why didn't you just say that then? Come with me."

She led Jimmy by the arm into the kitchen, where they raided an old junk drawer. Bertha withdrew a carving knife, which she passed to Jimmy before retrieving duct tape from another drawer. With quick work, she lashed down the top of Harold's urn before carefully placing him into her purse alongside the ammunition.

As Mrs. McFadden got ready to leave the apartment, she paused when she saw a rainbow bracelet around Jimmy's wrist. "I see you are a child of

God!" she exclaimed, mistaking his charm for the faith symbol it wasn't. "That's good. We're going to need an army of the faithful if we're going to save the world from the evil that's coming." Jimmy looked perplexed until his eyes landed on the pride armlet adorning his wrist.

He was just about to explain the real meaning behind his pride bracelet when Mrs. McFadden reached down and took ahold of both of his hands, bowed her head and said, "Let us pray to our lord and savior Jesus Christ for the strength we'll need to circumvent the coming apocalypse." Jimmy huffed, and rolled his eyes, and while he wasn't particularly religious, he figured that a bit of prayer ain't never hurt nobody, so he eventually lowered his head while Mrs. McFadden began her solemn recitation.

After finishing her prayer, Bertha looked down at Jimmy and said gruffly, "Alright, kid, spill the beans. I want to hear everything about this group of survivors." As she made her way out of the kitchen, the cacophony of creaks and groans from her protesting knees reverberated through the air like a poorly tuned symphony. It was like watching someone try to sneak up on a bag of chips. Jimmy followed closely behind, thinking to himself, *"I hope we don't need to make a stealthy getaway."*

Jimmy spoke softly as the pair gingerly entered the living room, and carefully navigated around the carcass of the Sally pig monster. "Mr. Livingston, who lives upstairs on the third floor, and my mom, who is working late tonight at Home Depot, have gotten to know each other well these past few months. I think they like each other. Anyways, Mr. Livingston has a minivan and said he could fit as many people into it as possible and drive us away from these creatures." He motioned towards the carcass of the pig monster. "But first he promised that he'd make a stop by the store to get my mom; I haven't been able to reach her since all this started." Jimmy drew in a shuddering breath and wiped away tears.

"I've chatted with your moms before. She's a tough ol' bird," Mrs. McFadden said with a gentle yet assured tone. "I'm sure she's just fine."

As they continued, stepping over and around the piles of splintered wood from what used to be Bertha's front door. Jimmy noticed the oppressive stillness that suddenly saturated the building like noxious fumes.

"Hold up," he said as he grasped Mrs. McFadden's cardigan to stop her in her tracks.

"What is it, boy?" she asked, reaching behind her and swatting his hand away.

Up until now, Jimmy had been acutely aware of the continuous racket coming from within the neighboring apartments, but within seconds, all had gone eerily quiet. Not even the faintest of murmurs could be heard from the group of survivors which had planned to meet on the first floor in a bid for safety and freedom. Jimmy's heart began to palpitate as he braced himself for what could be waiting beyond the threshold.

"Listen," he said. "Everything's quiet. Too quiet."

Mrs. McFadden finally took note of the unnatural stillness that had descended upon the building.

"Let's not draw too much attention to ourselves," Jimmy suggested, glancing down at Mrs. McFadden's popping knees. "Maybe you should let me go first." Bertha rolled her eyes but allowed the young boy to move ahead of her. Jimmy's blood ran cold when he saw a massacre beyond comprehension. Everywhere he looked, there were mangled corpses, and body parts which had been strewn across the walls, floors, and ceiling, like some macabre mural. The horror was almost too much for him to bear. His best friend, Reginald, who lived just down the hall, had been disemboweled with great vigor. His body lay carved open like a pig carcass in a butcher's stall. His intestines, which had been pulled from the ruins of his abdomen, snaked up and coiled around the banister like a gruesome garland.

Jimmy squinted into the darkness, straining to make out any distinguishable marks that may tell him where Mr. Livingston's van was parked. But the night was alive with shadows, dark and menacing figures that slithered along the walls and pooled on the ground, and he couldn't make out anything beyond the entrance of the corridor.

"Why don't you wait here while I slink out and see if I can spot Mr. Livingston or his van," Jimmy murmured. Despite Bertha's reluctance to let the child take a risk, the circumstances spurred her to consider the proposal.

"Listen to me closely, son," she ordered in a stern voice. "Be quick about it, and don't you dare take a step beyond the entrance of the corridor? Am I clear?"

"Yes, Ms. McFadden."

"It's Mrs. McFadden. Now scoot along, and hurry back."

Jimmy nodded his understanding, and once again peeked out the doorway to check for any signs of danger. Once he was sure the coast was clear, he cautiously crept into the hall and began to make his way towards the exit. The carnage surrounding him was enough to make his stomach churn and bile climb up his throat, but he did his best to keep his eyes averted from the mangled bodies, which lay strewn about like broken and forgotten toys. But the slippery ground beneath his feet was a constant reminder of the death and destruction surrounding him. He felt his resolve weaken for a moment and tears began to stream down his face when his eyes briefly passed over the body of Reginald.

Gritting his teeth, Jimmy steeled himself against the sadness as he carefully made his way through the gory labyrinth of shredded body parts. The wet squelching noise of his shoes on the blood-soaked ground was a stark contrast against the eerie silence. Every step forward seemed to take an eternity, as each footfall took him closer to his best friend's lifeless corpse. Jimmy took a deep breath to ready himself before he attempted to step over the partially eaten corpse, but he miscalculated the distance needed to bypass the body and his foot snagged on the ghastly garland of guts stretching from Reginald's abdomen.

Jimmy stifled a tormented scream as he crashed to the ground. Bile spilled forth from his nose and mouth when his hands plunged into Reginald's eviscerated belly, which was mauled beyond recognition. What was left of the boys' innards squelched through Jimmy's fingers as he urgently tried to eradicate himself from the cauldron of oozing entrails. After several attempts, Jimmy finally used Reginald's fractured ribcage for leverage and eventually pushed himself free. When his gaze dropped to his hands and forearms, a cry of revulsion tore from his throat - they were slathered up to the elbows in a gruesome mess of blood and guts.

Jimmy sat on the floor next to the body, crying silently. He desperately wanted to let out a loud wail of agony, but he was terrified of never being able to stop should he start. As his shoulders shook from the suppressed sobs, he hung his head and hugged his legs tightly. He almost screamed out loud when a gentle hand fell upon his bowed head.

Bertha knelt down on the ground and caressed Jimmy's trembling shoulder. "Honey, I'm so sorry. I should have never let you attempt this on your own," she said as she cradled the crying boy in her arms. "There, there now. No need to worry," she said warmly as she whipped off her favorite cardigan and began carefully wiping away the gore and grime from Jimmy's arms.

She tossed the stained sweater aside and wiped Jimmy's eyes with her fingers. "Feelin' better?" Mrs. McFadden inquired, to which she received a timid but affirmative nod. "Alright then, let's go take a peek at that getaway car."

Jimmy got to his feet and assisted Bertha in standing up. This time, she took the reins, taking Jimmy by the hand and leading him through the corridor, instructing him to keep his eyes trained on her back instead of the surrounding carnage. Without incident, they made it to the exit of the passage, only to be met with a shocking lack of a minivan that they were expecting. The remaining vehicles were a mystery to her, and she had no idea who they might belong to.

"Do you have any clues as to who owns any of these vehicles?

Jimmy scoured the parking lot with narrowed eyes. He deflated with a sigh and mumbled, "I don't think so. None of them look familiar." But then his eyes lit up. He pointed and shouted, a bit too loudly, "There. That's Hector's! He lives in the apartment directly above yours."

Bertha looked in the direction his hand was pointing, her gaze landing on an oddly shaped vehicle with two wheels on the front, and a single wheel on the back.

"What good does that do us?" Mrs. McFadden asked skeptically, to suggest they retreat into her apartment and hunker down until sunrise.

Jimmy's enthusiasm was palpable as he mentioned that Hector had taught him how to drive it. "We can go up to his apartment to see if he is still there. If not, maybe he left the keys behind, and we could borrow the bike in order to go and check on my mom."

"Are you suggesting that I let you pilot me around town on the back of a motorcycle?" Bertha asked incredulously. "Boy, have you completely taken leave of your senses?"

"It's a Trike." Jimmy spoke with deference, gazing at the vehicle. "Look at it, it's perfectly balanced, so there's no chance of it tipping over. Plus, this seems to be our only available mode of transportation."

Bertha looked at the foreign-looking machine and was about to veto his proposal when a loud screech, along with a chorus of squeals and snorts, startled the both of them. “And just how do you propose we get into Hector’s apartment?”

Jimmy gestured towards the gun that Mrs. McFadden had ready for action and replied, "We have a key.”

Mrs. McFadden and Jimmy retreated up the stairwell, Bertha's creaky knees echoing on each step as they made their way to Hector’s apartment. As they reached the top of the landing, Bertha surveyed their surroundings. While there were a few mangled corpses lying around, it was nothing compared to the bloodbath below. To their relief - but also their slight concern - they saw that Hector’s door was ajar. With her weapon in hand, Bertha pushed the door open to reveal a scene of destruction inside. The flickering of a tipped-over lamp illuminated the evidence of a fierce fight for survival. The noises Bertha had heard earlier in the evening now made more sense.

She examined the room between the disorienting flashes of light and caught sight of a gruesome image that she assumed to be Hector. The body, or what had once been one, was mangled beyond repair. Another flash gave her a glimpse of a set of keys lying on the kitchen countertop.

“I think I see Hector’s keys on the counter just inside the door. Wait here, and I’ll grab the ring quickly and be out in no time. Then we can go fetch your mother.”

Jimmy offered a silent acknowledgement and held his breath as Mrs. McFadden vanished into the apartment.

In-between lamplight flashes, Bertha carefully stepped over and around the body on the floor, inching her way towards the kitchen counter. She picked up the key ring, just as an eerie, child-like giggle echoed off the walls and brought her to a halt.

“Who's there?” Bertha whispered, turning sharply towards the sound. The lamp flickered, casting an unnerving glow on the room. In the brief illumination, Bertha caught only a glimpse of a ghastly creature that emerged from behind the couch. A three-and-a-half-foot-tall grotesque hybrid of human and animal. What was once a girl had been transformed into an abomination of nature - a living nightmare that shouldn't exist. Its smooth skin was now patchy with coarse hair, its once dainty fingers were bent and twisted and fused into hoof-like appendages, and its nose had turned into a piglet-like snout from which sprouted two tiny, but wickedly sharp tusks. Once again, darkness enveloped the room like a death shroud.

The lamp-light blazed, and the child-pig hybrid made a sound that was truly otherworldly. It was somewhere between a pig's squeal and a girlish giggle.

In the pitch, the creature rushed Bertha with ungodly speed. Another flash of light. This one, accompanied by a bang which echoed throughout the apartment, sent the monstrosity careening away from her where it landed in a fury of snorts, squeals, and feminine shrieks of fury. In an instant, the pig-child righted itself and made ready to charge again. Paying little to no attention to the gunshot wound on its shoulder. Before it could resume its attack, a flash of the lamp, followed by a shout of primal rage, illuminated Jimmy as he charged through the doorway, carving knife held high above his head. He rushed forward and, with a single, savage chop, sunk the blade deep into the beast's scalp. The whoosh of the knife slicing through fur and bone was accompanied by one final desperate screech as the deformed pig-child crumpled to the floor, dead.

"We need to get out of here, now!" Bertha said, making her way towards the doorway. "The noise of the gunshot is bound to attract the attention of more of those things."

They made it down the stairs and to the waiting Trike without incident. Jimmy hurriedly hopped onto the bike and started the engine.

"I can't believe I'm actually doing this," Bertha said as she made a sign of the cross with the gun still in her hand, prepared for whatever came next.

In an effort to avoid the heavy traffic on the interstate, Jimmy and Berta took a roundabout route, veering off onto back streets until they turned into Home Depot's parking lot, which was nearly empty, save for a van that looked like it could have been home to Scooby-Doo and The Gang. As the bike's headlights shined on them, Reby, Alberto, and Paula stopped what they were doing, unloading armaments consisting of machetes, hatchets, hammers, and even a chainsaw from a basket into the back of the van. Although slightly suspicious of their presence, the gang visibly relaxed when they realized it was only two people - an old woman and a young kid - on the bike.

So excited was Jimmy to be reunited with his mother that he quickly brought the vehicle to a halt, leapt off and called out, "Mom! Mom! I'm here!" as he urgently sprinted towards the entrance.

"Kid? Wait! Don't!" Reby screamed as she sprinted to intercept the boy in an effort to protect him from the unfathomable bloodbath he was about to encounter. It was obvious from the pile of mutilated store employees she and her companions had stumbled upon that the massacre had happened after closing hours. And painfully obvious upon hearing the heartbreaking sobs which ripped from the boys' lungs that he immediately recognized one of those corpses laid amongst the wreckage as his own mother. Jimmy collapsed onto his knees.

Bertha, sensing the concern in Reby's voice when she shouted for Jimmy, dismounted the bike, and hobbled towards him. She reached the distraught teenager and, with Reby's assistance, lifted him up off the ground and guided him away from the gruesome scene towards the back of the van.

The two women helped the boy into the van, and Bertha slid in behind him to find a young woman huddled in a blanket, looking terribly ill. Bertha gave her a timid smile, and though it seemed to cause her pain, the woman managed a small, weak introduction.

"Hi, I'm Genevieve."

"Bertha McFadden, and this here is little Jimmy," Bertha said in a sorrowful voice as she continued to console the sobbing child.

"Are you ok?" Mrs. McFadden asked Genevieve worriedly.

"I'm...okay. It's just been a difficult night," she responded through trembling lips, her face pale as death.

"Amen to that," Bertha uttered emphatically. "The Lord's grace will carry us through this valley of darkness," she said with pious conviction, her crooked fingers clasping the rosary beads still hanging around her neck.

Chapter Six

by Dorian J. Sinnott

THE OLD PICKUP RATTLED along the dirt road, blowing clouds of dust behind it. Though faded behind layers of rust, the stenciled lettering could still be made out on the doors: PIG PEN'S SWINE FARM. The engine revved as it sped up, struggling to accelerate. But still, it managed. Using every last bit of its energy to draw further from where it came from.

Gabe Shiflett fumbled for a cigarette, cursing beneath his breath. Shakily placing it between his teeth, he lit it, taking a long drag. The ash burned his tongue, but the rush of nicotine was enough to quell his nerves—if only for a brief moment. His dark brown eyes were glazed over, staring at what felt like an endless road ahead. Gripping the steering wheel, he didn't dare look back.

The heavy stench of blood and rot still invaded his nostrils. Even miles away from the farm, he could smell it. *Taste* it. Gabe swallowed a sob as he pressed his foot down harder on the accelerator. Pushing it to the floor. The truck strained, but he wouldn't let up. He longed for any chance to get as far away from the bloodbath that lay behind him. The carnage he knew would soon be making its way down the very road he traveled. Unforgiven. Hungry. Taking another puff on his cigarette, he heaved a shaky breath before reaching for the radio dial.

He flipped through the static of the stations, trying to ease his mind. Erase the images that played before him. Between the garbled screeching, the blaring voices of God fearing reverends called out. Spewing Doomsday allegations. Commanding those listening to pray. *Repent.*

"The end is near! Lift your hearts and souls to the Lord. *Pray* for forgiveness. *Pray*! From Acts 2:38, Peter replied, 'Each of you must repent of your sins and turn to God'..."

Gabe gritted his teeth against his cigarette. Frantically turning the dial, he continued scrolling through stations, heart racing in his chest. He wiped the sweat from his brow with the back of his hand, leaving behind a streak of blood. He was covered in it from head to toe. Some spots were still wet, the color of rust. Some dried in black blotches. Thick like ink. Taking one final puff from his cigarette, he flicked the butt out the window, letting the station he settled on crackle in and out of clarity.

"Incident at...Farm. Investigators say...tainted... Travis Sutherland...approximately... No reported survivors..."

Gabe dug his nails into the steering wheel, clenching his jaw. The hot tears pricked at his vision as he tried to maintain his focus on the road ahead. But with each word fading in and out of the static, he was met with visions of the farm. Of the bodies torn apart. Strewn across the fields. Caught in the barbed wire fences. Dumped in the pig pens for slop. But that wasn't the worst part. He ground his teeth at the thought of those monstrous abominations devouring the remains.

Half-man, half-pig.

He could hear their grunts and bellows in the back of his skull. Creeping down his spine. How they were drowned out by the begging and screaming of his fellow farmhands. Frantic, as they were ripped apart. Bones crunching and innards squelching. Staining the floors and fields in red.

His stomach lurched at the thought of the carnage. The flesh and guts hanging from those sharp tusks. Their beady eyes filled with rage. The sounds of their guttural squeals as they gnawed through ligaments and organs—grinding their teeth against bone. Gabe gasped a quivering breath, eyes wide and vacant. Each rush of air from his lungs became labored, his insides twisting into knots. It was the stuff of nightmares.

But it was real.

Unable to hold back anymore, he turned to the passenger seat, expelling a stream of vomit into it. The chunks sloshed, dripping down onto the floor as Gabe's chest trembled. He managed a whimper as the tears fell down his cheeks. With a shaky hand, he wiped away the traces of puke from his lips. It smelled rancid, but yet, it calmed his stomach.

Even with its putrid aroma, it was a refresher from the stench of decay. Massacre.

Static screeched from the speakers once again, causing Gabe to jump in alarm. As he attempted to ease his trembling breath, the news reporter's voice continued.

"Residents have declared a safe haven at a local Home Depot..."

The radio was clear now. Gabe snapped his attention back to it, freeing himself of his dark thoughts. Composing himself, he turned the volume dial up, listening to the rest of the report. News on the whereabouts of the sanctuary. A place he knew he had to head to.

As the intersection ahead came into view, he prepared to turn. Taking the road he hadn't planned on traveling, with the promise of safety.

Gabe was grateful to find a gas station on the outskirts of town. The truck was barely running on fumes at that point, and he knew he still had a distance to go before he reached his destination. Pulling up to the pump, he opened the door, hopping down. His feet scuffed through the dirt as he scanned the station—quiet. Vacant. He took a deep breath as he removed the nozzle, hitching it to his gas tank. He stood by for a moment, watching it fill, before turning his attention back to the convenience market attached. Wetting his lips, he pushed his hands into his pockets, starting inside.

"Hello?"

The interior of the station was just as empty as the outside. While the shelves were well stocked with canned goods, bags of chips, and magazines, there were no customers. Nor did there appear to be any employees. Gabe grunted as he headed over to the cooler, grabbing himself a bottle of water. As he approached the counter, he hesitated, then picked up a candy bar. Setting them on the counter, he counted through his bills, waiting for assistance. But it never came.

"Hello?"

Gabe's voice was louder this time. He leaned over the counter, looking on the off chance the cashier had fallen asleep behind it. But there was no one in sight. His eyes scanned the wall of cigarettes, landing on the packs of Newports. He wrapped his fingertips against the glass of the counter, growing impatient. His nerves were starting to get to him again, too. After another moment, he gave in, walking around the counter and retrieving a pack for himself.

He slapped it down on the countertop, peeling back the wrapper of the candy bar as he took a bite. Once again, he scanned the store. Waiting. Met only with silence.

His shoulders tensed, however, when he heard something from the back room. Behind the door marked with EMPLOYEES ONLY. His chewing slowed as his grip increased on the candy bar. Swallowing hard, his breathing became labored again. He turned his head towards the door, not daring to move otherwise. Listening.

All was still. Silent as before. Parting his lips, Gabe squeaked out a quivering breath.

"*H-hello?*"

A loud crash reverberated from behind the door. Stumbling away from the counter, Gabe wheezed. His eyes remained fixed on the doorway as a low, guttural growl rose up. A sound he had been all too familiar with. Snatching his water and pack of smokes, he backed away slowly—heading outside. Not daring to turn or look away from what he knew was waiting.

As he stepped onto the mat at the front of the station, another crash echoed. And then the door. Rattling. Slamming. Until it fell off its hinges—split down the middle. Hot tears rolled down Gabe's cheeks as he stood in shock, staring into the dark room before him. Into the eyes of the beast.

Its beady eyes blazed through the dim light, snout coated in fresh, wet blood. Its tusks were lined in flesh—tore clean from its victim. On the ground at its hooved feet was what Gabe could only imagine to be the cashier—a pile of torn innards and pulp. The face of the man had been gnawed clean off, skull crushed, and brain matter exposed. Gabe covered his mouth to keep from retching again. At his movement, the creature averted its gaze to him, exposing its yellowed teeth.

Swallowing hard, Gabe took another step back—slowly. Then, once outside, he bolted for the truck. The human-pig hybrid screeched in furious hunger, bursting through the doorway and into the store. Cans and shelving units toppled over beneath its force as it slammed against them, breaking out into the lot. It was even more hideous in the light of day.

Fresh blood coated its body, a thick saliva dripping from its mouth. Green mucus coated its wet nose as it snorted, blinking back the brightness of the sun. When its eyes adjusted, it focused on the farm's truck, and Gabe—searching the bed.

He threw the burlap and blankets to the side, rummaging beneath the toolbox and rope. His hands trembled as his heart raced, fingers frantically fumbling through supplies. The sounds of the beast approached, louder than ever, as he cursed aloud.

"*Shit*!"

Popping the toolbox open, he breathed in relief at the sight of a small box of bullets. He shook them free, snatching the rifle from the truck bed beside him. His hands shook as he loaded it, sweat beading on his forehead.

"Come on..." He stumbled through the process. "*Come on...*"

Once the bullets were in, he cocked the gun, turning to the side of the truck. The head of the creature popped over it, jaws opened wide. A hot, rancid breath erupted into Gabe's face as he gritted his teeth. It began clambering over the side, squealing as a string of saliva blew from its mouth. Gabe leaned back, mustering a quivering whimper as he pulled the trigger.

BAM!

A stream of blood and guts rained down into the truck bed. Gabe flinched as it covered him, still holding the rifle out as a precaution. What had been the head of the pig monster was now splattered open—like a smashed pumpkin exposing its innards. Its eyes rolled around momentarily before another rush of hot air escaped from its mouth. And then down it went.

It landed beside the back tire of the truck, hitting the ground with a *thud*. Black blood pooled from its opened head, oozing out into the dirt. Gabe steadily lowered the gun, shoulders trembling as he fought for air. His eyes were wide, fogged over in shock. When he finally was able to compose himself, he sat forward, leaning over the side of the truck. He stared down at the body of the creature—unsure if truly destroyed or simply stunned. Gripping the rifle tight, he carefully slipped from the bed and climbed back into the driver's seat.

His heart raced as he gripped the steering wheel, vision fixed on the road ahead. He bit his lip hard, easing his thoughts before reaching for the radio dial. This time, a tangy tune rang through the speakers. Upbeat. Exhaling, he shifted the car into drive, pulling away from the pump. He kept his thoughts on the music and the signs before him. His tension eased. It wasn't much farther to the place of salvation. The safe haven the news reporter had spoken of a place he could hide. Relieve his mind. Gather resources.

"That is," he thought, "unless they've already made it there, too."

Taking a deep breath, he pressed his foot to the gas, peeling out onto the main road. The sun reflected off the hood of the truck, blinding him momentarily. But as he sped down the dirt road towards his destination, he peered into the rearview mirror. The body of the beast remained where it was—strewn out in a bloody heap under the heat of the sun. Left for the elements. For whatever would choose to come along and deliver it the same fate it had dealt to humanity.

Chapter Seven

by C.I.I. Jones

A Piggy Interlude

Ah, Jesus. My head's burning. It's the only thing I have felt, actually experienced, for the last—well, I don't know how long. I'm living a hellish nightmare. I can see my hands thrust out in front of me, only they're not hands. It's like my fingers were fused into two pig digits. They hurt like hell, these pig hooves. I can feel my teeth, my tusks, burrowing into the flesh, and the slops of meat and gouts of blood, and strands of innards slipping down my gullet without tasting. But I'm not doing it. The pilot in my head is. Maybe the same little guy who gouged a gas nozzle through my eye socket and let er' rip on full blast, then lit a match inside my skull. The fever burns like my brain is the throne of hell. And the pilot, a tiny little piglet, tells me where to go.

I try howling at the moon.

The piggy-pilot screeches a response inside my head.

PIGS DON'T HOWL YOU PIG FUCK!

So, I squeal at the moon.

I tear off into the night. My heaving breaths are a hybrid. Sometimes it sounds like it always used to–the labored breathing of an out of shape man who did far too little jogging in my day-to-day life. Sometimes it's the starved husky breaths of the animal erupting out of me. I have no idea where I'm running to. Food, more than likely. I could have my pick of the strewn corpses that litter my suburban street. Flashes of memory come back. Hot dogs on the grill. Ketchup dripping from a pork-filled bun, then my snout burrowing into the split open side of my coworker's wife, tearing her open as easily as one of those split open hotdogs. The comparison of her long intestines to sausage links sends a drivel of bloody saliva down my chin. Then blackness.

I don't stop for the easy meal of my dead neighbors. The piggy-pilot and the fire in my head tell me to find something running, something living. And now, those are the only voices I listen to. Squealing and running. Mad with fever and hunger.

I don't know if it's been hours or days that I've run. I do know it feels like it's been a lifetime since my last meal. There are others like me, but we are no pack. We are a new evolution, and we all want to survive. In my frantic journey for a feast, I've seen more than a few of these pigs gutting each other for one last morsel of meat. We are a brutal bunch with no commitment to our own. And I have been bested, again and again. I feel like another pig has come to life deep in my guts and he is trying to eat his way right through my innards, destroying me from within. That's hunger. Hunger like I've never felt in my life, and between that and the fever, this new reality is all I've ever needed to be convinced that hell is indeed very real. I'm living in it.

But, My God! I see them. Most of the humans have managed to barricade themselves away. Us pig-fucks have to figure how to get to them, a tall-order given our new unwieldy and cursed corporeal forms. But, to see a whole group of healthy humans right out here in the open, well, it's like the hand of God has split through the stormy ceiling of hell, to reach out to me. Then that same God points that way, like the host at a Golden Corral, showing the way to the choicest meats.

Go! Fucking Go!

Piggy-pilot screams from the fiery void where my brain used to be.

They're a long way away, though. Several hundred feet. And I am evolving every moment. I've been hungry long enough to know that it's not always wise to listen to that starving voice inside my head; the one that's always screaming, *FEED, PIG-FUCK! FEED!*

So, I slowly trot to the shadows off to the side of the building. A full-frontal assault has yet to net me a meal. It has gotten me battered by would-be victims. Or the commotion of the hunt has attracted others just as starving piggies that overpower me and take the meal right out of my mouth. An attack from the shadows will serve me better. From the darkness, I can hear them. They speak amongst themselves, words I can barely comprehend any longer. A language that I once spoke. Now, all I know are the squeals banging around in my head.

"Careful with that, Jimmy!" one of them screams. It's an old woman, fat. I never ate ass in my old human life, but here is a full meal of it in the form of this old bitch. She's tugging some sort of bag out of a young man's hand. "My Harold would just be devastated if he knew I'd let his remains be handled so roughly. By some..."

"Hey, what the fuck!" a girl calls out from the back of the van. She's young and her face is flushed.

"It's okay," the kid says. "I know Bertha doesn't mean it."

"I was just going to say kid," Bertha mutters as she tucks the bag a little closer to her ample bosom. Her look says that she didn't mean *just kid* at all. "Honest, I hadn't even thought once about him being black."

Jimmy's eyes go wide, but he waves a calming hand to the red-faced girl.

Inside, piggy-pilot screams, *EAT BERTHA'S BUTT! EAT IT NOW! SLURP HER INNARDS STRAIGHT THROUGH HER ASSHOLE! EAT BERTHA'S BUTT!*

I let out a faint squeal to try to temper the roiling in my belly and head. It's too loud. Another woman, this one long and slender, barely dressed, pokes her head from the sliding door of the van. "What the hell was that?"

"Was what?" another guy says as he slips from the driver's seat. He walks toward the loading dock the van is parked near and picks up a box. He huffs under its weight as he lugs it back to the van. "I didn't hear anything. But I'm spooked. Let's get the fuck out of here. Any more supplies we need to load?"

"Does Home Depot carry any proper clothing?" Bertha crows. "Miss Genevieve seems to be in need."

The good-looking lady, Genevieve, I gather, looks off into the shadows where I'm hiding, and it takes everything in me not to run straight at her and rip one of those long, sexy legs right off the stem. Like a flower petal. I wait, though. The hardest thing in the world to do. But I have to wait, or I won't eat, and if I don't eat, the fire in my head and the hunger in my belly are going to meet in the middle at my heart, and they will demolish the poor, decrepit organ.

They work on for a few minutes longer, pulling various objects off the loading dock and throwing them into the van. There are six of them. I don't get all their names–just Jimmy, Bertha, the fat piece of roast, and Genevieve. I've snuck closer and closer, a specialty that is not in the pig's usual skillset, so it is slow going. After ten minutes, I've moved a long way, within twenty feet of my next meal. Bertha hasn't contributed much to the loading of the van, just barked orders, most of which are ignored.

"I think that's it," the other boy says. "Everything a person needs to survive the end of the world."

"All that and the love of our savior," Bertha says. She pats her bag.

"Let's load up," Jimmy says.

Genevieve continues looking off into the dark. We are practically locking eyes. I can smell her cheap perfume from where I stand, that mingles well with her sweat. The girl that got all red-faced over Bertha's veiled racism comes up, pats her on the back and whispers, "Let's go."

Genevieve nods and is ushered back to the van and jumps inside. Bertha waves everyone to their seats, then she bends down. The last one in, ready to go, but she's trying to brace herself to lift into the van. Her beautiful, fat ass is poking up and the screeches of the piggy-pilot are unignorable.

FEED YOU DUMB PIG FUCK! FEED RIGHT NOW!

I squeal loud and hard as I rip out from between the shrubs I've been hiding behind. I can feel the blood and meat from my last, long forgotten meal, gurgling out of my throat, regurgitated in the excitement of this next hunt, this next kill. There is a collective scream from the van as the group realizes an attack is imminent, but it's too late. Blood is about to be spilled. There's nothing to be done about it now.

I erupt from the shadows like a bullet. My hunger is the gun. That plump ass, still bouncing back and forth as the fat bitch tries to pull herself through the door, is the target. I angle my head now, intent on putting my left tusk directly into her asshole, ready to perform a rudimentary, savage colonoscopy. I hear her gasp in horror, then suddenly she swings around. It's a knee jerk reaction, a last instinct springing her to survive.

The bag swings with her, a violent arc that travels like a baseball pitched with professional speed and precision. I hear the shatter before I feel it. Thick glass clatters inside her bag. I snort loudly, and when I do, a fine powder shoots up my nose. I'm choking on dust that solidifies the bloody coagulate already trying to spill from my gullet. I'm coughing and choking. Louder than the demands from the screeching piggy-pilot to *feed, feed, feed*, I hear Bertha wailing.

"Oh God! My Harold! God forgive me, my loving husband!"

The dust wafts from her handbag and all around my head as my vision clears and I lift myself up on my rear hooves. I cough and hack, spitting up a thick quick-crete style mixture of blood and dust. My attack has been a failure, initially at least. As I regain my senses, the fire in my head hits a fever pitch, and I know I will tear this old cunt to pieces.

"Hey! Little pig!"

I jerk my head in the direction of the yelling. The world swims with the violent motion. If a pig fuck like me can get concussions, I am severely concussed. There's Genevieve, standing at the head of the van, her long legs looking like two drumsticks.

BUT I WANT THAT RUMP!

I look back toward the van door to find Jimmy hopping out, grabbing Bertha's bag, and pulling the old woman up through the sliding door, all in one swift motion. I charge forward with another guttural squeal. But the kid, Jimmy, is digging around in the dust caked purse. My hooves try to catch up with my mind, and what I'm seeing. Jimmy yanks a gun, a real cannon, out of the handbag, lowers the barrel, and blasts three earth shattering shots in my direction. I feel a slug burrow into my shoulder and when I look down, I'm surprised to still see the arm in place. I am bleeding, though–like a stuck pig. I have no intention to stop, but when I look back up, the door is slamming closed. The piggy-pilot is going haywire.

YOU PIG FUCK! YOU MISSED HER! I HOPE THESE FUCKERS SPIT YOU AND ROLL YOU OVER AN OPEN FLAME!

I'm horrified and the knots in my stomach constrict with hunger pains. I stand up to my full height, something I've never done in this new, hellish body. I tower over the van. I hear Genevieve scream, and I realize not all is lost. She's scampering around the front end of the van when I go for her. I stretch my legs out, really testing this new body, discovering this evolution of a new, true apex predator. And I know that the group has found their sacrificial lamb. She will not outrun me, and there is no bag of dust or pistol that can save her.

One hoof reaches for her throat, and she runs into it like a rope snag. I wrap my other hoof around and pull her off the ground. It's difficult, with no fingers and a hole the size of a fist through one shoulder, but I manage. I hold her up so that we see face-to-face. The look of horror in her eyes is nearly contagious. Even I am afraid for a moment. Afraid of what is happening. Afraid of this new body and what I am about to do. Her fear pricks something at my core that is clinging to my last shreds of humanity.

FEED! EAT! CONSUME! SATIATE! NOWNOWNOWNOW!

Whatever empathy I feel doesn't dig down deep enough. Not far enough to mute the necessities. And even as I hear the van doors open and see a flash of light in my periphery and feel another slug tear through my center, I know I have to eat. It's my only choice. I burrow my rotting teeth into the fattest vein I can find in her throat, and I pull. The sound of Genevieve's flesh rending is like the splitting of overstretched leather. A shower of blood rains out of her and soaks me, the van, and Genevieve's would be savior in a blanket of crimson. I push my face in for another bite and feel the strands of flesh sliding down my throat. I feel like a kid caught with my hand in the cookie jar, but unable to resist. I know my hand will get slapped, but I NEED the cookie.

The slap comes in the form of another thunderous gun shot. I drop the woman and she collapses in a heap on the pavement. I stumble back a few steps, and on two toes instead of five, while losing a lot of blood, I can't keep my balance and fall to the ground.

There is some clattering from the survivors. They all run toward Genevieve, who I know is already dead. If they were smart, if they had their own piggy-pilot guiding them from a hellish command center in their own brains, it would be telling them to get away, and get away fast. Now! But they are not predators, and they are not animals. All of them seem unable to just get in the van and run. And that may be their own undoing.

At least, I intend to make it their undoing.

The damn bleeding heart fools are too concerned with a dead carcass to see me pulling my bloodied, hole-shot body off the pavement. A couple are making their best efforts at first aid, but even my fried brain knows that's like trying to slap a Band-Aid on a severed limb. I put my head down while they flounder. There will be no squeal this time. There will only be tusks and the parting of flesh. I charge.

KILL! KILL! KILL!

I'm practically on top of them, a fifteen-pound bowling ball chucked at top speed, about to pick up a strike. I'm drooling, their meat practically in my mouth. I'm so laser focused that I hardly notice the beam of white light I'm suddenly bathed in. I hardly hear the screeching of tires or the smell of black exhaust farting out of the nearby pickup. I do, however, feel the crunching of steel into my pink, mutated flank. I feel every bone in my body shift as the truck crushes me and sends me through the air, more like a pig stuffed animal than a mutant pig monstrosity. My face pounds into the concrete and I can feel my flesh tattered with bacon. It's suddenly hard to breathe.

For a moment, my human mind comes back, loud and clear. My conscience. It's here to let me know that I'm dying, and that's probably a good thing. It's telling me to close my eyes and sleep. The last thing I see before I go is a man jumping from out of the driver's seat of the truck that has killed me. A cig dangles from his lip. There's a gun in his hand.

"I'm Gabe!" he shouts, and he's running toward me, practically skipping with joy from the task at hand. But I'm already dead and all is darkness before the gunshot rings out, splitting the skull open on my exquisite piggy corpse.

Chapter Eight

by D. A. Latham

The Beginning

Pig Pen spit his tobacco on the ground as he watched the silver sedan pull into the driveway in front of his house. No one ever came up to his house. Well, except for his farm hands, that is. "They must be lost." He thought as he watched two men in grey suits exit the vehicle. They both had sunglasses on and the one who got out of the passenger side carried a black briefcase.

"Ya'll lost?" Pig Pen shouted at the men.

"Are you the owner of this pig farm, Sir?" Briefcase man asked.

"Sure am. What's it for you?"

"We have a business proposal for you. One I think that you will be very interested in."

"Oh? I will, huh?" Grabbing ahold of the straps of his overalls, Pig Pen glared at the men.

"Absolutely. May we come in?" They didn't wait for an invitation. Walking up the stairs onto the porch, they entered the house and waited for Pig Pen to follow them.

"I s'pose, since you're already in, I could listen to what you have to say. Let's go sit in the kitchen."

The three of them entered the small kitchen and sat down at the yellow, warped table. Briefcase man opened the case and pulled out a small portable DVD player. He inserted a disc and pushed play. Turning it so Pig Pen could see the screen, he let the video play.

"Specimen 12344-99, given Super Grow three times a day. Age 4 months. Weight 285 pounds. As you can see from the before picture on the screen, the subject at age 3 months was just 100 pounds. In thirty days, she has gained 185 pounds and is now ready for slaughter. Note the markings on the sow's back, snout, and right front leg that indicate this is the same animal as in the picture."

The video played for a few more minutes, showing the grotesquely fat pig waddle around an enclosed pen. Its movements were slow and labored, as the super-fast weight gain on her small body hindered movement.

"You see, Mr..... Uh, you never did tell us your name," Briefcase man said.

"Just call me Pig Pen. Everyone else does. What are your names?"

"Our names don't matter, Pig Pen," the quiet one said with a hint of hostility.

"Right. Okay, Mr. Pig Pen, Super Grow can accelerate the growth of your hogs in record time. Faster growth, faster to slaughter, faster to get money for the meat," Briefcase man stated.

"And how would this benefit me?" Pig Pen asked, chewing on the wad of tobacco in his mouth.

"Boleous Labs would like to supply you with Super Grow free of charge. We need to have a client that can show true results, not just results in a lab, so that we can market this to other farms. It has already passed FDA approval and is ready to be distributed. But we think that no one will be willing to buy from us unless they can see that it truly does work. You'll get free feed for your livestock, which will increase their size faster, allowing you to send more to slaughter, and that all equals more money," quiet man said.

"Free, you say? Well, shit, I'll take anything for free. Sign me up!"

"Excellent!" Briefcase man pulled out a manila envelope and removed the papers inside. "If you could just sign on page three, we can have your first shipment out here tomorrow."

"Hoo-weee, this is gon make me loads of money!" Pig Pen squealed in glee as he signed the papers. He didn't bother reading it. Well, if truth be told, he could barely read anyway. Slamming the pen down onto the table, Pig Pen smiled at the two suits. "So, what time should I expect the delivery?" He grinned.

GABE SHIFLETT DIDN'T UNDERSTAND why there was another delivery of pig feed. They had just gotten a few tons delivered last week, which would last them a month. But, if he wanted to keep his job, he unloaded the truck and stacked the sacks of feed like he was told. When it was time to feed the hogs, Pig Pen had told him to use the new feed first, which didn't make any sense. They should be using the older stuff first. Shrugging, he loaded up the troughs and called the pigs to their breakfast.

He always liked watching the pigs eat. They were hilarious as they fought for spots at the trough. Those cute pink faces buried snout deep in the feed never failed to make him smile. Some would say he was too fond of the pigs to be working at a pig farm when he knew they would be slaughtered, but it was just the way of life. And, well, Gabe sure did love bacon!

"Hey, Pig Pen, what's this new feed?" he asked as Pig Pen came over to make sure the pigs were eating up the new feed.

"This new feed is gon make me a lot of money. It's guaranteed to make these pigs get bigger faster so I can send them to slaughter sooner."

"Get bigger faster? How?"

"Don't know. Some fellas from a fancy lab-ora-tory came to see me yesterday and offered this new feed to me for free. I guess they want to use me for advertisin' or something," Pig Pen shrugged. "Don't matter to me none, free feed saves me money. Even if they don't get bigger faster, I still come out a winner."

"Don't you think this could taint the meat? Make it not suitable for market?" Gabe protested. "There was already that issue with the tanker truck that crashed near here the other day. Remember how the water turned all green, and we didn't realize it until the whole herd had been drinking it for a few days? I'm sure that wasn't good for them either. Did the company that owned the truck ever tell you what it was?"

"Nah, they wouldn't return my calls, but the pigs seem just fine. Ain't nothin' to be worried about. Probably just some of them fancy sports energy Millennial drinks........." Pig Pen said. "After they done with this feed, let's get them weighed. I want to keep a close watch on their progress. They'll be weighed once a week. Understood?"

"Sure thing, Pig Pen. Sure thing," Gabe said. He had a bad feeling about this new feed.

Careful records were made of the pigs' weights. Sure enough, in one week, all the hogs in the group given the Super Grow feed had already gained fifty pounds. As the rotund creatures hobbled around the pen, Pig Pen saw nothing but dollar signs on hooves. He was happier than a pig in shit.

Gabe, being skeptical of this miracle feed, watched the hogs closely. After three weeks, he noticed some of them developed yellow sores on their skin. Their noses continuously leaked brown mucus. And their eyes were bloodshot. Their aggression increased as well. Two sows started fighting at the trough one day, Lila and Betsy. When Betsy didn't move out of Lila's way fast enough, Lila attacked, goring Betsy with her tusks. As Betsy lay bleeding out in the muck, Lila began chomping down on her. The sounds of Lila eating brought the rest of the drove over and they all devoured Betsy in a manner of minutes. As the corpulent beasts finished, there was nothing left of the two-hundred-pound Betsy but blood covered bones.

When he brought this up to Pig Pen, he was told to be quiet about it. Pig Pen promised him a huge bonus once the pigs had been sent to slaughter, and he received his payment. He knew Gabe could use the money. His old pickup was on its last legs. With the bonus, he could buy himself a brand-new truck and help out his ailing momma with her mortgage. This was too tempting to Gabe, and he agreed.

Two weeks later, the pigs were ready to be sent to slaughter. Gabe, Pig Pen, and another farm hand began to load the hogs into the trailer so that they could be driven to the slaughterhouse. A total of twenty-five hogs were set to go. They would be slaughtered and their meat sent to grocery stores all across the country.

Gabe and Pig Pen used the pig boards to herd the drove onto the ramp into the trailer. They were being stubborn and began biting at each other. Pig Pen reached in and used the electric prod to get them moving.

He leaned a little too far into the chute and one of the pigs bit his arm, tearing into his flesh.

"God damn mother fucking pig!" Pig Pen yelled as he beat on the sow that had bitten him. "Look at my fuckin arm!" Swinging his injured arm out of the chute, blood splattered onto Gabe's shirt.

"Stu! Help Gabe get these hogs in the trailer!" he yelled at the other farm hand. "Damn sow bit me!" Pig Pen pressed his other hand over the gash in his arm to try to stop the flow of blood.

After loading up the hogs, Gabe went up to the house to check on Pig Pen.

"Pig Pen, you alright, man?" he yelled as he entered. He walked into the kitchen to see Pig Pen wrapping his arm with gauze. "You need to go to the hospital? That was a pretty bad gash."

"Nah, I sewed it up myself. Don't need no doctors." He answered as he finished securing his bandage. "Sure does hurt like a bitch, though!" Pig Pen grabbed the bottle of whiskey from the table and took a long swig.

"You look awful pale. I really think you should go to the hospital. Maybe get a tetanus shot or something. Those pigs were sick, man. You don't know what they had, you could get it too."

"Shut up, Gabe." Pig Pen stood up and suddenly bent over as a horrendous cramp seized his insides. He grabbed his stomach and dropped the bottle of whiskey to the floor. "Unph!" he grunted, doubling over.

"Pig Pen? What's the matter, man?"

"My...fucking...stomach...is...cramping up," Pig Pen wheezed.

He started to shake, and Gabe could see sweat start pouring down his face. Abruptly, Pig Pen spewed rancid smelling vomit all over the floor. The brown puddle grew larger and larger as it flowed towards Gabe's feet. Pig Pen collapsed to the dirty kitchen floor as he lost control of his bowels and hot liquid shit spurted from his ass. His jeans were no barrier as the bloody feces were forced through the fabric and sprayed the cabinets. Convulsions overtook Pig Pen's body and coarse hair started to grow on his face.

"Jesus H Christ, what is happening?" Gabe yelled.

Pig Pen looked up at Gabe and reached out a hand. His eyes were bloodshot, with the crimson fluid leaking from his tear ducts. "Help me!" he pleaded as he tried to crawl over to Gabe.

Gabe backed away from the contorting figure on the floor. He watched in terror as Pig Pen's face began to elongate, his nostrils widened into a snout. Pig Pen opened his mouth and tried to speak, but all that came out was a long, sorrowful squeal. His body began to enlarge, the skin turning a shiny pink and bursting from his clothes. Tusks pushed through his gums, making blood drip down his chin.

Pig Pen stared horrified at his hands as they morphed into hooves. Bristly hair ruptured from his follicles in sparse patches. The pig-man stood up on his cloven feet and let out the loudest roar-squeal that shook the house and had Gabe wincing in pain at the sound. Terror flowed through his veins like ice water. His bladder let go and warmth dribbled down his leg and filled the air with the acrid scent of urine.

The half-pig half-man stalked towards Gabe, snorting and grunting. Gabe turned and ran from the house. The sound of the beast's hooves clomping over the wooden deck spurred him on as he reached his truck. Heart pounding, he shoved the key in the ignition, started the truck, and peeled out of his parking spot. The pig-beast galloped after him, but something must have caught its attention because it abruptly changed direction and headed towards the pig barn. Gabe was relieved that the creature was no longer following him.

Gabe felt a drowning sense of guilt from allowing the pigs to be sent to slaughter. If a bite from one of the infected pigs could turn someone into a grotesque beast, what would happen when someone ingested the meat? He would have to return and kill the remaining hogs to make sure they didn't get turned into meat that could mutate humans. He needed a plan. He would go home and get his gun, then go back, and take care of the problem. He could only hope that something would happen to the truck before it reached the slaughterhouse.

"Good Lord, what have I done?" he whispered as tears streamed down his face.

Boleous Labs Top Secret Memorandum

Re: Super Grow Feed Project

From: Project Chair Dr. Daniel Hoftenfluss

To: Board of Directors

The growth enhancing serum that was developed to be put into the Super Grow Feed was obtained from an unidentified organic substance that was found in the Amazon Rainforest. This substance, when applied to flowers, increased their growth and bloom production substantially. Later, it was applied to tomatoes with the same effects.

After much debate, it was decided to start trials on animals. The enzymes were broken down and injected into mice. The mice began to grow in size within a matter of weeks, but there was no increase in aggressive behavior. The trials then moved to fish, with the same results.

The goal of this project was to increase food production to counteract the horrible effects of hunger and food cost inflation. The next trial was to focus on a farm animal. This is where we decided to begin testing on pigs.

Specimen 12344-99, after being given Super Grow Feed three times a day for a period of thirty days, has not only exhibited increased growth but has also exhibited increased aggression. The specimen gored two research assistants as they attempted to draw blood samples. They died and were eaten by the specimen in a matter of minutes. The footage of this incident from the security cameras has been erased and all record of the two employees has been purged from our databases.

Re-examining the organism during the pig trials, it was discovered that the organism was an unknown virus. Microcellular examination of tissue from pigs that were given the Super Grow Feed showed that the unknown virus had taken over the cellular make-up of the animal, mutating the animal from the cellular level. There is no way that could be good for human consumption.

One ton of Super Grow Feed has gone missing from inventory. Two low-level lab technicians have disappeared, and it is assumed they are responsible for the loss of the Super Grow Feed. The government has sent a damage control team to locate the technicians and the missing inventory.

Project Super Grow Feed has been suspended effective immediately. All specimens and research materials will be destroyed.

-End of message

Chapter Nine

by Megan Stockton

Paula was sitting quietly in the passenger seat as Alberto weaved around vehicles and bodies in the streets. He was breathing out of his chapped lips, leaning over the steering wheel with his arm wrapped around the upper curve.

"You know where we're going?" Reby asked, peeking over his shoulder through the cracked and dirty windshield. Alberto looked over at Paula out of the corner of his eye, making sure she wasn't looking at him. And then he muttered, "Fuck no..."

"Didn't think so," Reby murmured in response.

All Alberto knew was they needed to get out of the city. Smaller population, less opportunity for... zombie-mutant-boar things. They could get somewhere, gather their bearings, and figure out the next step. They needed supplies, and they needed more information. That was the most important thing: information. Information was *power*, and they needed a lot of that right now.

There was a groan from the back of the van: the sound of someone who may have been asleep and made a satisfied little noise in their throat. A little moaning hum that wasn't even a conscious decision, just an adorable little grunt.

But then it escalated. It became a painful wail that made Alberto's head spin. It filled him with a nausea that he could only attribute to apathy, imagining what hurt somebody must have been feeling to make that kind of noise.

Reby disappeared and Paula suddenly turned to look back, plump hand going white-knuckled against the gun in her lap.

"Y'all, there is something wrong with this girl," Bertha said, pressing her back into the door of the van. "Oh, there's something bad wrong. This is *unholy*, Lord. Please put your arms around us in a protective embrace."

Alberto could barely see her face in the rearview mirror, just enough to recognize the terror there. He couldn't see Genevieve at all, but he knew that she was sitting behind him. He felt her pushing against the seat, writhing as Reby tried to hold her down. Her feet made paddling sounds and her screams were becoming higher pitched and husky.

"What is going on back there?" Alberto asked, voice shaking. He mashed the gas further to the floor, driving over a body and sending the entire crew lurching upwards. The van made a revving sound in protest.

"What's going on with her face?" Jimmy squealed. It was the first Alberto had heard his voice since he'd gotten in the van. He had been shell-shocked and delusional overseeing the body of his mother. Now he sounded sober and *terrified*.

"Move away, son," Bertha demanded.

There was a faint click.

"What are you doing?" Paula asked. "You can't fire a gun in this vehicle!"

She had unbuckled now and was turning around to face the back, rounded buttocks taking up half of the front seat, beehive hair smashed against the roof. Her own gun was now lying across the seat, almost venturing into Alberto's lap.

"You put that weapon down, you daft woman!" Paula continued.

Alberto had a cold sweat pouring from his brow now as he listened to the cacophony of voices rise in volume.

"*Shut the fuck up!* Somebody tell me what..."

Then Alberto realized what was going on with Genevieve. Rising up behind him in the rearview mirror, he saw the bubbling flesh and distorted limbs. Genevieve was growing, transforming. The van was suddenly filled with the aroma of pig and excrement.

Alberto knew, somewhere in the logical portion of his brain, that he should stop the van. There were monsters running around the town: massive towers of gelatinous flesh with wiry hair, destroying everything they came into contact with. How was Genevieve becoming one of those things? *How?* Why now? He wanted to pretend it wasn't happening, because he couldn't rationalize it.

But instead, he kept driving, pushing himself backwards into the seat and mashing the pedal to the floor.

Bertha had the gun in her hand. Alberto knew without looking back to see the glistening barrel, because she was still screaming for Jimmy to move away.

"Jesus Christ!" Reby exclaimed, diving onto the floor as Bertha fired.

The sound was impossibly loud inside the van. Alberto's ears started ringing and his vision exploded with bursts of red and black fireworks. The scent of gunpowder and something hot now joined the existing *eau le porc*.

It took him several seconds longer to realize that he'd been hit with fragments from the shot, his right arm suddenly leaden and heavy with pain. The wheel jerked as his arm dropped and he struggled to recover with the other hand.

Paula had fallen backwards at the sound of the gunshot, clutching her face with her hands.

"Lord, my eyes!" she wailed, pressing her fingers into her sockets as she leaned against the dashboard. "That bitch has shot out my eyes like little Ralphie Parker!"

Someone else was screaming, but Alberto couldn't tell who it was. Reby? The kid? Was it Alberto himself? He was lightheaded, but he needed to steel himself. He couldn't pass out now.

The mutated Genevieve suddenly lunged towards Bertha, and the two collided against the door. The gun went off again, but this time through the roof of the van. Bertha was somehow holding her own against the massive creature. She had a hand on each tusk, wrestling the beast's head away from her with all of her might. She was red-faced and flustered, roaring back at Genevieve's tusked face.

Alberto could hear Jimmy calling Bertha's name now, voice wet and sobbing. With a loud clatter, the door popped open, and Bertha and Genevieve were gone. Jimmy dove towards the door with his hand out, but Reby grabbed him around the waist, sloppily tackling him as she struggled to keep him from bailing out of the door after Bertha.

Alberto looked back in the mirror, watching as the pig monster bounced across the highway, Bertha's body totally obscured by its massive form. She'd surely been crushed. No one could survive that, could they? And even if she did... Even *if* she did, that fucking thing would be pissed off. Genevieve would tear her to ribbons, and she'd be nothing more than a pile of assorted bits on the asphalt.

"Stop the car!" Jimmy demanded, freeing himself of Reby's clutches and clambering over the console.

"Kid..." Alberto snarled as Jimmy tried to jerk the wheel out of Alberto's good hand.

"Stop it!" Reby lurched forward, pulling Jimmy's hands away, but it was too late.

Alberto was already losing control of the van. It veered to the left and across the other lanes of traffic, jumping a curb. Alberto slammed on the brakes, but the van's forward momentum kept it going. He didn't think it ever even slowed down as it barreled down an embankment and came to rest at the bottom.

The airbags exploded in a cloud of white dust, pressing its aggressive softness into Alberto's face. He fought against it, pushing it until it deflated. He touched his now sore nose before clutching his wounded arm.

The interior of the van was quiet, and Alberto was afraid to look at anyone else. He clenched his eyes shut, taking slow breaths in and out of his nostrils as he waited for a sound, any signs of life from his three unrestrained passengers. When he heard nothing, he first stole a glance over at Paula. She was lying in a crumpled heap, face planted against her seat where she had sat backwards-facing and on her knees. She looked smaller, somehow even more vulnerable and innocent than she had before. He noted that her chest still rose slowly, softly.

He then looked into the backseat, but there was no one there. At some point, Reby and Jimmy had been thrown from the vehicle. He found himself both relieved and panicked. Satisfied that he didn't have to look at their mutilated bodies, or that he didn't see one of them lodged through the windshield from being a human projectile in the crash. Terrified that he might find them dead somewhere out there, thrown from the van and then hit, or just dead from the impact to begin with.

Or, *maybe*, even worse: not dead. He couldn't get them out of here, not injured. This place was crawling with monsters, and they were still a little ways from freedom.

Alberto *had* to find them. He struggled with his seat belt, fumbling with his nondominant hand as he tried to click the stubborn button to release him. He had never prayed a day in his life, but he was praying then. As he crawled out of the van and stumbled onto the muddy embankment, he prayed that Reby was alright. He prayed that she was at *least* alive.

"Reby!" he called hoarsely.

He thought he could hear something a few yards away, maybe a muffled and weak *over here*, but he couldn't be sure. Maybe it wasn't Reby at all, maybe it was Jimmy's voice, or even Bertha's (if she'd somehow survived).

"I'll be back for you, Paula," he whispered into the door, trudging to the back of the van and towards the distant voice. That was when he saw movement at the top of the embankment, where they had left the highway.

Towering over him like a monolith of flesh, not-Genevieve stood looking down at him. She had twelve nipples, each set getting larger and sagging more the higher they were. Her thighs were powerful and thick, nearly as wide as Alberto's entire body. She could outrun him easily. There was absolutely no chance for him to even try to get away. He started backing up slowly, maintaining eye contact with the pig as she stared down at him, nose twitching wildly. She snorted, sending a cloud of snot and saliva into the air. She grinded her teeth, bowing her head as she raked one hooved foot against the pavement. Alberto swore he saw sparks fly from the contact.

"Alright, piggy piggy piggy..." he cooed. "Easy, pig."

He just needed to get to the passenger side door and try to find Paula's gun. He didn't know if he could figure out how to use it, but what choice did he have?

"Alberto?"

Now he was positive he'd heard his name. His heart leapt in his chest as he came to the passenger door, fingers finding the handle. He stole a glance to his left, finally seeing Reby as she lay on the ground. She looked beat up pretty badly, but she managed to say his name one more time and he saw her look up at Genevieve. He knew that she was aware enough to realize what real danger they were in right now.

"Slowly, Alberto..." she croaked, not moving anything other than her lips. She didn't even blink.

Alberto wound his fingers around the door handle and pulled it open. As soon as the door popped, Genevieve was on the move. She let loose a war cry, charging down the embankment nearly on all fours. She was *pissed.* Alberto dragged Paula out of the car, and she sprawled out onto the dirt snoring. Her gun was on the floorboard, but the crash had damaged the dashboard so badly that he couldn't reach it.

"Alberto!" Reby was screaming now, and Genevieve was in such a close range that he could smell her.

He pressed his shoulder against the dented dash, fingertips brushing the wooden grip of the gun.

"Come on, come on, come on..." he whispered to himself.

And then he had it.

He pulled the gun out and aimed it at Genevieve, taking a deep breath as he prayed again. This time for Jesus to work this damn gun because he sure as fuck didn't know how to.

Chapter Ten

Steve L. Clark

ALBERTO'S FINGER CURLED AROUND the trigger, and he aimed the gun at the charging beast that used to be Genevieve. She snarled, raising one long, clawed arm into the air. The mutated creature closed the distance between them quickly, and when she was only three feet away, Alberto fired.

He had aimed at her head, but his quivering hand betrayed him, and the bullet smacked into the creature's neck, ripping a chunk of graying flesh into the air. It didn't stop the beast, but it caused enough pain to make her twist away. Instead of being eviscerated by the massive claws, the Genevieve-monster collided with him, shoulder first, sending them both to the ground. Alberto gasped as the wind gushed from his lungs. Upon impact, he heard a crackle of bone within him, and the sudden throb of pain confirmed at least one broken rib.

The pig beast's momentum caused her to flip over him and roll deeper into the embankment, but she was rapidly on her feet again. Blood oozed from the gaping wound in her neck, but it showed no signs of slowing her down. She let out a guttural roar and charged at Alberto.

"Move!" Reby screamed.

Alberto groaned and tried to stand, but a stab of pain rippled through his midsection, dropping him to his side. He could hear the thundering pounds of the creature's hooves approaching, and he looked at Reby.

"I'm sorry," he said, with tears brimming. Defeated, he closed his eyes and waited for the end to come.

A cannon blast split the air, and his eyes snapped open. Gabe stood a few feet away, shotgun in hand. The next thing he knew, the Genevieve-monster dropped in a heap beside him. Alberto rolled away, grimacing at the pain. The beast twitched and grunted but could not stand. A pool of dark blood formed underneath it.

Gabe approached cautiously and aimed the gun again. “Get back,” he ordered, nodding toward Alberto.

Alberto scooted away until his back pressed against the side of the van. He sat holding a hand against his busted rib and watched Gabe fire again, this time at point blank range into the back of the creature’s head. Brain matter and viscera burst in a pinwheel of gore around the thing, and the beast lay motionless.

Silence enveloped them as the ringing echo of gunfire faded. Reby climbed to her feet and jogged shakily to the van, dropping beside Alberto.

“Are you okay?”

“No, but I’ll make it,” Alberto said. He struggled to his feet, groaning with each movement. Reby slid under his arm and helped him stabilize.

“She dead?” Gabe asked. He pointed the shotgun toward the van where Paula’s body sat slumped in the seat.

“She wasn’t,” Alberto said, “but I don’t know about now.”

“Where’s Jimmy?” Reby asked.

Gabe nodded toward the road. “Saw him up there. He was banged up but looked okay. Saw that thing coming for you, so I didn’t get to check on him. We need to get him and get out of here. We made a lot of noise. If any more of those things are around, they’ll be coming.”

Reby nodded. “I’ll go with you. Alberto, you stay here and check on Paula. We’ll get Jimmy and come back. Then we’ll decide what to do next.”

“Go on,” Alberto said. He waved her away and walked gingerly toward the van’s passenger door.

Gabe and Reby jogged up the embankment and peeked out onto the road, looking for any sign of approaching pig beasts. The road was clear except for Jimmy. They spotted him some forty yards back up the road, sitting on his knees next to a heaped figure.

Bertha.

As they approached, they could hear the soft whimpers coming from the boy. Reby dropped beside him and put her arm around his shoulders. He turned to her and fat teardrops streaked trails down his cheeks.

"She's dead," he said. "My mom is dead, and now she's dead, too."

"I'm sorry, Jimmy," Reby said. She knew he was right. Bertha lay on her back, blank eyes staring at the sky. Her face was relatively unmarked, but blood had oozed into a pool around the back of her head. Reby suspected if they lifted her, they would find her skull busted open.

"I didn't even know her that well. I don't know why I'm so upset."

"We're all upset, kid," Gabe said. He walked a few steps away, turning his back. "Me, most of all. I might've been able to stop all this from happening, but I didn't try. All this blood, it's all on my hands."

Reby turned and stared at Gabe. "How could this be your fault?"

Gabe gritted his teeth. "I knew there was something wrong with those pigs when they went to slaughter. I could've told somebody. Somebody besides Pig Pen. I could've done something before it was too late. But, I didn't. It all happened so fast."

"Listen, man," Reby said, "I get you've got some guilt about all this, but as fast as the world got fucked, I really doubt one farmhand could've done much to stop it. I don't know all the details, and right now, we don't have time to dig into it. We have to get off the road and get somewhere safe. Maybe once we've done that, you can empty your soul and ask forgiveness. For now, you've bailed us out more than once, and that's good enough for me."

Gabe gave a tight-lipped smile. "You're right. I can feel sorry for myself later. Let's get back to Alberto and Paula and figure out our next move."

Reby stood and motioned for Jimmy to follow her.

"We can't leave her here like this," Jimmy said. His tears had stopped, and a fierce determination filled his red-rimmed eyes. "Not in the middle of the road. What if a car comes? We can't leave her here to get run over."

"She's dead, kid. It doesn't matter, now," Gabe said.

"Yes, it does. Help me move her. Just to the side of the road."

"Fine," Reby said.

Gabe shook his head in frustration but hurried over to the woman's body. Jimmy and Reby positioned themselves on each side of her, both grabbing hold of an arm. Gabe grabbed her ankles in each hand, and on the count of three, they lifted Bertha off the road and shuffled over to the edge, then lowered her gently onto the grass.

"Thank you, Mrs. McFadden," Jimmy said. "I might not have made it out of the apartment building without you. I'm sorry this happened."

"That's sweet, kid," Reby said, "but we really have to go."

"I know." He sniffed and wiped his eyes with the back of his hand. "I'm ready."

The three of them jogged back down the road toward the van. Alberto was propped against the passenger door. He turned to look at them as they approached, a grim expression on his face.

"Doesn't look good," he said, then nodded into the van.

Paula still sat huddled and unconscious in the passenger seat. Her breathing was shallow and irregular.

"I can't wake her up," Alberto said.

"Shit." Reby paced back and forth beside the van. "What do we do? We can't leave her, but we can't stay here."

"We're not going anywhere in the van now, either," Alberto replied.

Gabe waddled up the embankment and peered up and down the road, then came back. "Way I see it, we've only got one option. We can't carry her with us, and we can't leave her behind. That means some of us have to go try to find somewhere safe or another car, while the rest of us stay here and protect her. Alberto's in no shape to be running, so you'll have to stay here."

"I'll stay with them," Reby said.

Gabe nodded, then turned to Jimmy. "You good to come with me? We'll have to be fast and quiet."

"I can do it. I'm on the track team at school. I'm fast."

"Good." Gabe reloaded the shotgun and handed it to Reby. "Can you handle this? I'll take the handgun. Easy to carry on the run." He scanned the ground, then saw the pistol laying in the grass where Alberto had dropped it when the Genevieve beast had plowed through him. He snatched it up, checked the chamber, then shoved the weapon down the back of his jeans. "We'll be back as soon as we find a car or place to hole up."

Reby nodded. "Be fucking careful."

"Yes, ma'am," Gabe replied. "You ready, kid?"

Jimmy gave him a thumbs up.

"Let's go."

Gabe and Jimmy ran up to the road, scanned for any sign of approaching pig monsters, then headed south.

Reby watched them go until they vanished from sight. She sucked in a deep breath, then let it out in a long exhale. Alberto climbed gingerly through the open sliding door of the van, stifling a moan as he twisted and lowered himself into the seat.

"Probably shouldn't be outside, Reby. If one of those things comes along, you don't want it to see you."

"I'll be careful. If one of those fuckers comes along, I want to see it before it sees us. No more surprises."

They settled into silence. Reby moved carefully from position to position, peeking around the frame of the van, using it for cover. Once, she thought she heard the sound of a motor in the distance, but it faded just as quickly.

"You think we're gonna make it out of this?"

Alberto's voice startled her. Reby considered his question, thought once to lie, then thought better of it. Alberto would hear it in her voice. "I don't know, man. The way things are going, probably not."

Alberto chuckled. "That's what I like about you, Reby. You're always so positive. A ray of fucking sunshine."

"That's me," Reby said.

SQUEEEEEEEE

Reby's eyes bulged, and she pressed herself against the side of the van. Another squealing roar sounded from above them on the road, back the way they'd come. Reby looked frantically at Alberto, who lifted a finger to his lips.

Quiet, he mouthed.

Reby strained her ears. The squealing had stopped, but now she could hear a wet, tearing sound mixed with slurps. The noise was steady but didn't seem to come any closer. Slowly, she took deliberate, cautious steps away from the van, staying low and keeping the shotgun in front of her. She heard Alberto whisper at her to stop, but she pressed on. When she'd gone far enough to see the road, she froze.

The beast perched on all fours over Bertha's body. It had used a tusk to eviscerate the old woman's torso and rooted its snout vigorously in her entrails. Reby felt bile rising in her throat as she watched in revulsion. The monster slung its head back, dragging a mouthful of intestines with it, chomping savagely.

Reby ducked and slowly backtracked down the embankment, never taking her eyes from the edge of the road. She couldn't see the beast now, but she didn't want to take a chance by turning her back and risking being surprised. Get back to the van and stay out of sight. Hopefully, the creature would finish dining on poor old Bertha, and go on its way. They just had to be quiet and have a little luck.

Reby was halfway down the embankment when she heard a gunshot from the south. She froze, aware that the snorts and slurps from the creature had also stopped. Then came a second blast. She heard the beast scramble to its feet and take off at a wild sprint, hooves knocking furiously on the pavement. She lay still on her stomach and watched the gore-soaked creature disappear from view, charging in the same direction Gabe and Jimmy had gone.

She couldn't know for sure that the gunshots came from Gabe, but she thought it was likely. Wherever they were, she thought they were in trouble.

And more trouble was coming.

Chapter Eleven

by Anton Cancre

"THE FUCK WAS THAT?" Alberto blurted out to Paula's still unconscious form. His voice was too loud. What if something out there heard him? What if that something wasn't deterred by fiberglass and steel? His busted rib screamed in electricity and fire as his breath hitched. At least Paula was smart enough to keep silent. Damn girl would probably outlive all of them in her quiet oblivion, the way things were going.

Something thumped on the roof of the van. Several somethings. A rain of light bump-skitters enveloped the vehicle. Alberto had an easy view of the windshield from the seat. All he had to do was move his head a bit to the side. Open his damn eyes. Whatever was falling on and around the van would be right there. A few muscles tightened. A few others loosened. That's it.

But he didn't want to. He really, really did not want to see anything. There had been too fucking much already. He was done. He was safe. He had to be. He just needed a little of time. A little bit of rest. A short break from this insanity to get himself back together. He wasn't scared. He was just tired. That's all. Tired.

Paula groaned accusingly from the passenger seat diagonally from him.

"Oh, fuck you," Alberto muttered. Then he forced his eyes open. His first thought was tribbles. The sky was raining small, fluffy tribbles. It made at least as much sense as anything else that had happened tonight.

Then he saw the feet. Little adorable jellybeans pressed up against the glass. Heard the light scritch of claws on metal.

Cats. Too many cats for him to count were running through the culvert and over the van. Dogs, too. Like every stray in the whole damn city had decided to run a marathon. His brain didn't know what to do with the image of so many cats and dogs running alongside each other without fighting or at least barking and hissing.

"I'll be damned. Venkman was right."

The words fell out of his mouth, alongside a flood of laughter. Each contraction of his chest hurt like a son of a bitch. It didn't matter. He needed to be quieter. Who knew what might hear and come to investigate? He just barked out heftier laughter. The intrusive hope that Gabe and Jimmy had their rabies shots, being in the path of this miraculous exodus, didn't help matters.

Something quiet in the far back of his head whispered about a movie he'd seen once. A tunnel. A broken-down car. A sea of rats descending on our intrepid survivors. More importantly, what they were running from. The whispers did nothing to quiet his laughter, though. The exploding agony of his side and the raw burn in his throat made no difference, either. His laughter came faster and heavier. It filled the van with a manic roar.

Then he saw them.

There were no individuals. All that he saw was a dark, uneven wall rising up from behind the flood of animals. Small stars flickering from within it. A rustle of fine spikes, like crab grass grown too tall, along the top. It was growing far too fast and way too high to be more cats or dogs. His lungs froze mid laugh, all sound cut off as suddenly as flipping off a switch.

He didn't need to see the details. Moonlight glanced off glistening snot that ran from flared, forward facing nostrils. Furrowed brows of skin overflowing itself. Raw, seeping pustules leaking thick yellow ooze. Thick pink folds of skin over dense muscles. Sparks jumping from the scrape of keratin against concrete. Cruel jutting lower jaws. Splatters of blood and chunks of human and inhuman offal hanging from vicious tusks. Not just the one or even ten he had seen in the streets, but a legion. Multiples of tens. Probably multiples of hundreds behind them. A full block party that just found out the neighborhood shithole has wings for a buck apiece and five-dollar pitchers.

Alberto knew what they were. He knew where they were going and he knew what they would do when they got there. He knew, with one hundred percent certainty, that, if these animals built by both millennia of evolution and centuries of intentional selective breeding for speed and agility could not escape those beasts, there was no universe in which his under exercised, injured ass stood a snowball's chance in hell of evading them. The knowledge settled an unfamiliar calm over his mind. In the face of inevitability, his fear faded away into a numb certainty. With that certainty came a plan.

He wouldn't lock up like he did when Bertha pulled the gun and Genevieve turned. He would act. He would be smart this time.

There was no getting away, but there was an opportunity to hide. To distract them. If he moved fast enough, maybe they wouldn't have a need to tear their way into the van. Maybe, just maybe, if he did things right, he could trick them into thinking that there was no need to go after him.

Locking the doors was as pointless as keeping them closed. Those things would tear through the van as easily as he could tear open a box of tissues. He slowly, quietly, opened the sliding door across from him. The cats and dogs still streaming by didn't try to scramble in, but he wasn't worried about any that might. They'd be an easier meal for the beasts, if it came to that. The breeze that rushed into the car cooled his sweat and comforted him, whispering to him that everything would be all right.

"Shhhhhhh," he said as he reached diagonally towards Paula. "I'm glad you're still asleep. You don't have to worry about any of this. It'll all be okay for you. You can rest."

There was a moment where he was worried. When he grabbed onto her shoulder. Would she stir? Would she yell out and bring the whole horde of pig beasts down on them before he had a chance to fix anything? Paula could still fuck everything up for both of them.

The moment passed, though. Her breathing stayed steady. She didn't move. Her eyes stayed closed. Even when he picked up her arm and hooked a hand under her armpit. When he started lifting up and pulling her towards him, her head lolling around on her neck reminded him of the time Jake got piss-blind on that shine he bought from Pig Pen a few years back. Even after it burned a violent orange and they all warned him that it was probably at least half radiator fluid, the idiot tossed back the whole damn Mason jar.

His head flopped around the same way when Alberto, Janice, and Martine lugged his incoherent, gibbering ass into the emergency room of Saint James Infirmary. Okay, he finally admitted to himself, not so much *inside* as *at the door of.* Jake was okay. Ish. Slurred for a while and never could remember his phone number afterwards, but who the hell memorizes their damn phone number?

"You know," Alberto said when Paula's head flopped in his direction, "I'm honestly a bit jealous. You took a smack to the back of the head and then... blank nothing."

As he pulled her back toward him, he slid out of his seat onto the floor of the van. He didn't move the seat back. Keeping his space close was important. Paula was so small. Much smaller than him. He'd have to make himself small. Having less space to work with would give him no choice.

There was a moment when her shoe caught on the armrest of the seat. Why didn't he think to put it up first? This was some basic idiot shit here. Luckily, an arm wrapped around her midsection and a yank backward freed it. Paula's body felt much heavier than he expected when it landed on him. An elbow jammed right into his already fucked up rib, lighting up his brain and almost making him pass out. He was definitely going to have to get back to working out when this all smoothed over.

"It's okay, Paula," he told her as he straightened her body over him while pulling himself into as tight of a fetal position as he could under the circumstances. His shins pressed painfully against the metal of the driver's seat. Something plastic and hard jutted from the seat behind him into his back. Paula's body lay flat against his arm and side, forcing the knob on the inside of his elbow against his injured rib. He wouldn't break, though. He could tough this out. Pain was just a series of nerve signals to tell his brain something was wrong. He already knew that EVERYTHING was wrong. With his top arm, he reached around and straightened out Paula's legs, splaying them along the floor of the van. The goal was to have her cover as much surface area as possible.

"Just rest now, Paula," he whispered into her ear. The cacophony of squeaks and grunts, and hooves scraping against concrete and metal overtook the entirety of Alberto's existence. He briefly hoped that the last of the cats and dogs had gotten away. Or that any leftover slow or lame ones would have the decency to distract the porcine horde. "You're better off this way. The rest of us'll have to hide and cower and scrabble to survive this. You get to rest. You don't have to know any better."

A snuffling came. Too loud and too clear to be outside of the van. Alberto had the time to wonder whether or not it might have been smarter to leave the door closed. Maybe they wouldn't have smelled her musk. Or his fear. Or the raw, splattered meat coating the back of the van. They might have just wandered on by, enticed by the easier prey of animals out in the open.

It was too late now, though. All he could do was slow his own breath. Become nothing. Not even another corpse. Just a stone. Just more metal holding up this bag of enticingly warm, moist meat. Something, it or the inevitable they, didn't need to pay any heed to beneath such a supple and available meal.

It squealed.

Loud and desperate.

Hungry.

Voracious.

Joyous.

An avalanche of other squeals joined in. The frenzy began. He could hear them fighting among each other. Elbowing and kicking. Biting. Keening. Desperately trying to cram themselves into the meager space provided by the door. Flat, stony teeth clamped against one another, grinding dentin to dust in the air.

There was a hollow thump and tear. A high-pitched screech of metal stretching and tearing. Triumphant howls and gurgles. Pained wails. A chaotic symphony of noise and rage and hunger. The dry scrape of cracked glass and bone.

Then, so much more weight than Paula could possibly have borne in her slight frame. Shaking. Shuddering. Pulsing in violent undulations of frenzy.

Alberto knew she could not have awakened. She was too far out of it. Those airbags pack too much of a punch. They can kill a kid facing the wrong way. That's what the diagrams on the display made clear. Surely it turned off every active part of her brain. She had to have been dead already. An inactive squiggle of fatty gray tissue that didn't even know enough to turn off the muscles that were supposed to keep it running.

She couldn't feel the squelch and rip of skin and sinew. Those hitches and spasms she passed along his side were only from the beasts digging into her. There was no way that they were her own last agonized breaths.

He was doing her a favor. He saved her from running. Saved her from hiding in the night. Kept her from a bare existence, hoping that no new monsters would find her while she dug roots up from the soil in a desperate hope for a few calories to keep her going another mile or so.

As the thick wetness poured over Alberto and the weight of predator and prey pressed down on him and the beasts slurped noisily at fat and tore at foot upon foot of loosed intestine and the stench of bile and shit mixed with the sourness of pig-man sweat, he thought only of how much better off Paula was and how sad his fate was, to have to carry the burden of her sacrifice into whatever remained of the future of his life.

Chapter Twelve

by Cat Voleur

There'd been days in track where Jimmy had felt like he was running for his life. The pressures of his team depending on him to beat his best time, the potential for a scholarship, the promise of making his mom proud; they had all gotten to feel awful heavy sometimes. When he'd struggled to breathe, there was nothing he could do but run faster. He'd known damn well he couldn't stop until he crossed the finish line, or it would all be over. Actually running for his life? Well, it wasn't anything like he'd always thought it woulda been.

His eyes burned from the chemical smoke in the air, and his nostrils were filled with the stench of the orange sludge that had spattered onto his chest when that thing had been shot in front of him—like bacon grease left in the heat to rot. There were screams and squeals echoing through the night from so many directions that Jimmy didn't know which way to turn. Metal threatened to burn his palm. It was... oddly freeing.

There was nothing to do but keep going. No thoughts. No anything. For a time, Jimmy thought he was running alongside cats and dogs and rats, and that seemed to make as much sense to him as anything else that was happening. It wasn't until after the stampede dispersed, and he'd turned left at the bottom of the hill, that he had started to slow. His legs ached, and there was a stitch in his side, and he was greedily sucking down mouthfuls of that putrid air. He realized that despite it all; he was smiling.

For a minute he'd forgotten about his mom, and about Bertha, and Gabe. *Gabe.* The manic, toothy smile faded from the young man's face, and suddenly the street felt that much emptier. The gun felt very heavy in his hand.

Everything had happened so fast. They'd found another vehicle, pulled to the side of the road, doors open. Gabe had been the one to stick his head in and then ... *then.* Before Jimmy had known what was happening, the man was pointing a gun at him. He'd barely had time to put his hands up before the shot had gone off–not *at* him, but at the thing *behind* him. By the time he'd turned around to stare, it had drawn even closer.

For the second time that day, he'd been hoisted up by giant, monster-hooves. The creature hardly seeming to notice that it was spewing thick, chunky blood out of the open wound left by the first bullet. The second shot came from the creature's side at point blank range, popping several pus-filled sores open into Jimmy's face, but it still hadn't let go. 'The head!' Jimmy had wanted to scream at Gabe. In games and movies, you always had to aim for the head. But when he'd opened his mouth to say so, he'd gotten his first taste of the yellow fluid and suddenly he was retching into the monster's gnashing teeth.

He didn't see how the rest happened; it seemed like only a second before he was on the ground, gasping and gagging on all fours as he tried to collect himself. Gabe had been between him and the creature, which had been squealing and thrashing with all of its fading strength. The farmhand had been bloodied and defeated as he had pressed the gun into Jimmy's hand. "Run," he'd ordered.

Jimmy had wanted to protest, to thank him as profusely as he'd thanked Mrs. McFadden earlier when she had saved him from one of the creatures, but then they'd heard something coming. Another loud squeal, and what had sounded like a tidal wave of incoming paws. When Gabe had ordered him a second time to go, Jimmy had just gotten up and gone.

Now, of course, that he found himself alone, he wished he hadn't. There was no thunderous sound of hooves still chasing him, but Jimmy had no way to meet back up with Gabe–who had very possibly just sacrificed himself. Jimmy wasn't sure, but he thought that he'd seen a chunk of flesh torn from Gabe's shoulder as he had turned over the gun.

Was it a bite? Jimmy tried and failed to remember if the wound had looked more like a bite or a scratch, not sure how much it mattered. He took stock of his surroundings, more than a little surprised to discover just how far he'd run. He knew he could always go back, to try to help Gabe finish whatever needed to be done before it was too late. Maybe it would be easier, safer at least, to try to make it on his own. The decision was heavier than the gun, which he gripped for courage before taking off: his mind made.

EVERY SECOND FELT LIKE an hour as Reby held her breath. She wasn't sure which of the terrifying noises had kept her alive, but she knew she wouldn't be safe crouching where she was forever. She needed to know what happened to Jimmy and Gabe–if they had been the source of the gunshots. Even more urgently, she needed to make sure that Alberto and Paula were okay. She hated that her retreat had caused her to lose sight of the two.

She raced back to where she'd left them, her shoes squelching in the viscera that had been left in the wake of the rampage. Her heart sank when she saw the van, the metal sides practically shredded from the dented frame. There was a trail of meat. Stretchy intestinal fabric had been pulled from the wet puddle of human remains in the center of the vehicle to the hole in the roof, catching on the jagged metal edges.

"Alberto," she whispered, not wanting to believe it.

"Reby...?"

She almost screamed when she heard Alberto's voice pipe up from the hole. The top of the van had dented in so much that she hadn't even realized there was still space for a person behind the driver's seat.

"You're alive?" she asked incredulously. Relief washed over her.

"Are you?"

She didn't bother answering. She just reached in to help pull Alberto out of the mess. He winced in pain, which was when she remembered about his rib. She hoped that was still the worst of his injuries because his clothes were soaked through to the point of dripping. His skin was crimson and tacky to the touch. She succeeded in getting him about halfway out of the wreck.

"What happened?" she asked.

He looked her over carefully, as though she were the one drenched in blood. "Where did the pigs go?"

"There were gunshots before they took off, the one that was eating Bertha and... and it sounded like maybe another one." Reby wasn't sure about that last part. There had been so much commotion while she'd been hiding, holding her breath, just waiting for the worst to pass. It would have been smarter to run, but she was gladder than ever she hadn't left him behind. "Were you hurt? What happened to Paula?"

Alberto looked down at the slick, red interior of his surroundings, and Reby's heart plummeted. Paula hadn't always been her favorite person in town, but she'd been good in the end. Strong. Tougher than expected. She didn't deserve whatever it was that could turn a human into pulp.

"Help get me out of here," he said.

There was something not right about his voice. He didn't sound like himself. Reby remembered all those days at the hospital, when one half of his face had still been bandaged to hell, and he had tried to turn her away. That was practically the first time she'd seen him sober since he first got busted for weed back in freshman year. Fuck, that felt like a long time ago. He'd sounded older during those visits, ancient, detached. That had still been better than this.

"Tell me what happened with Paula," she tried again, but she wasted no time in helping to pull him out the rest of the way.

He gritted his teeth together and grunted as he got to his feet. Reby thought his legs would buckle, and he'd keel over, but he stood steady if not exactly straight. His body curved, hunched protectively around his injured side, and he began to walk.

"Alberto," she insisted.

"I tried to help her," he said.

"And?" Reby walked beside him, her arm stretched out behind his back, ready to catch him in case he did fall.

"I didn't," he said flatly.

It was like talking to a stranger. There was no emotion whatsoever in his words. "Tell me the rest of it."

She didn't like going in circles like this. He'd never made her do that before.

He let out a terrible, wheezing sigh, and his head hung so low that gloppy strands of hair completely obscured his face. It was a wonder he could see where he was going enough to step around the debris that littered the streets. She knew they were traveling south, down the same street Gabe and Jimmy had gone. "One of those things grabbed her. I tried to pull her into the backseat. It tried to pull her out of the van. I guess ... well ..."

Reby was less put off by the mental image of the little old church lady being ripped in half than she was by the tone of Alberto's voice. She'd become desensitized to the senseless violence and gore over the course of the night, but she'd never be used to the sound of her best friend lying to her. Alberto was, well, he was everything that she had left in the world. Mopey, self-indulgent, smart ass that he was, he had never been good at lying. She could count on one hand all the times he'd bothered to try.

"I don't believe you."

He gave a pathetic, lopsided gesture that might have been a shrug, and didn't look back. "You don't have to believe me."

This was exactly what he'd done, before his release. When she had first tried to see him. He'd given one half-hearted lie about what had happened to his stoner friends, and then he'd gotten evasive. It had taken her weeks to get any semblance of the real story out of him, and that had been so damn fragmented and surreal that she hadn't known what to make of it. They didn't have time for all that bullshit now.

"If you're trying to protect me from something, you can knock it the fuck off."

"I'm not," he said coldly as he lumbered down the street. And she believed him.

It made a sick sort of sense. What could he possibly have seen in the time she'd been gone that would be worse than what they'd witnessed together? Nothing. Unless he was trying to protect himself.

"Stop," she said, but he didn't listen. "Hey, seriously. Slow down a minute, would you?" But when she pulled away the arm that she'd hoped to steady him with, he kept going. "I'm not sure you should be walking around in this condition."

"It's fine.""Doesn't it hurt?"

"Not really."

She let him pull ahead several paces in front of her so she could get a proper look at how he moved. His limping motions were jagged. Each footstep fell heavy onto the pavement, and yet it looked like even a breeze would be enough to knock him over. He was trembling head to toe, clearly unwell.

"You're shaking," she said as she slowly started to resume walking, keeping what she hoped would be a safe distance. "I know you're in pain."

"Did you ever think...maybe pain's not real?"

"What?"

"I mean. Our eyes aren't really interpreting things as they are. Are they? It's all just... chemical reactions in the brain, trying to make sense of the world around us. Nothing's real. If you think about it."

"What are you talking about?"

"That's what Damien said. That's the sort of shit he was saying, at the end. That nothing was real." His voice quavered.

They hadn't talked much about it. About Damien. Or David. Or Michael. The ones who had died that first night. Reby had been curious, but content to wait until he was ready to talk about it. Only now that he was opening up, she was pretty sure she didn't want to hear it.

"You don't have to think about that now. We've just got to find Gabe, and Jimmy, and–"

"He was tripping balls, talking about how things weren't real, and our molecules never make contact. And then ... something ripped him and his fucking *molecules* all to pieces."

Reby was pretty sure she hadn't seen any bites, or new tears in his clothes, but underneath all that blood, how sure could she be? She watched the haggard way he persisted forward and considered the resigned tone in his voice. Those things must have been close to him before they'd gotten Paula. Close enough to bite, probably. And why would they have left him there if they'd seen him? Unless he was already turning. "Why are you telling me this?"

He stopped moving, finally, when he crossed the street at the corner. She got as close as she dared, still several paces back. She didn't want to believe that Alberto could be infected, turning into one of those things, keeping such a secret, but nothing about him seemed right.

"It's times like this that show us what we are. What we're made of. I guess, before these ends, I just want someone to know–"

His voice was drowned out by the loud squeal of something from down the street beside her, and Reby didn't have to look to her right to know what it was. "Run!" she screamed, quickly closing the distance between herself and Alberto. Gabe and Jimmy had been traveling faster than them, but not for long. And one of them should still have the gun that had fired. If they could only make it that far–

She felt more than she saw Alberto leaning in as she passed, and for just a moment, she slowed. She'd help him lean over onto her, she'd fight off the fucking pig beast for him–hell, she'd *carry* him if she had to. It only took that one moment of hesitation for his foot to snake between her ankles, sending her face-first into the concrete.

There was the blinding heat of the flesh being grated from her face as she skidded to a stop, and she'd barely had time to process what had happened before she was being torn backwards again.

Crunch!

Something in her ankle cracked and then her whole leg was lit up in agony as she was dragged back further, her body anchored to the decaying pig-hulk by its massive teeth that punctured her broken bone. She smelled the cloying, rotting breath of the creature before the white tunnels of her vision came into enough focus that she could see the gargantuan form of the thing over her shoulder in her periphery. Her fingers scraped and bled down to the black-polished nubs of her nails as she clawed desperately to get away.

Another sickening crunch resounded in her ears as she was yanked further into the beast's maw, and she screamed so loud that she almost missed the faint sob of the fumbling, fleeing man ahead of her. "I'm sorry," Alberto whimpered. "I'm so sorry."

As her body started to go into shock from the pain, she forced herself to twist and face her end head-on. The pig was massive, but it was on all fours, further lost to the transformation than the ones they'd seen lumbering around on two legs. She could use that. It took another noodly slurp of her leg, already gone to the knee, and she took her one chance to brace herself on her good side as she was pulled closer. She sat up. Her hip pressed into the disgusting, bubbling snout of the creature, staying it for just a moment. It was enough. She summoned every last ounce of strength and plunged both of her balled fists into its eyes.

They popped like grapes, and she was rewarded with twin fountains of grayish, yellow fluid pouring over her. The howl was loud enough to alert Gabe, or Jimmy, or whoever might be left in their piece of shit town, that the sow was coming. She didn't think it would give much chase to Alberto now that it was blinded, but she couldn't be sure. She wasn't entirely sure she cared.

She saw at the end, as she bled out, exactly who her friend had been.

Chapter Thirteen

by David Simms

"I SAW WHAT YOU did."

Alberto stopped walking towards Jimmy, just for a fraction of a second, but it was enough to prove what Jimmy thought. He didn't see him leave Reby, but watched the aftermath, a scene of bloodthirst he doubted would ever wash from his memory.

They managed to meet within the train station and bolted the door behind them. The gigantic porcine hellions pounded on the steel doors, hoping to gorge themselves on both men.

"Her knee," he replied, without a tinge of empathy. "She complained about it when she saw me. I told her about Paula and how I tried to save her. Said she banged up her leg, running away from those pigs."

Jimmy's words wouldn't come. A swath of emotions swarmed in his head, from confusion to rage to disgust. How could Alberto do that? The bastard didn't have the balls to see how she died, or her own heroic final act, because he ran.

"Yep," he managed.

"By the time I realized she had fallen, I heard the screams."

Yet she didn't scream. Not at all. Just one guttural howl of fury at the monstrosity that killed her. By blinding the fucker, she likely ended its terror, but she'd never see it happen. Jimmy watched her die as the pig stumbled away and tumbled into the ditch, shrieking in agony.

"Got it." His eyes burned into the other man. He had to say something, otherwise he might go after Alberto right then and there.

"Okay," Alberto said, obviously ignoring what both men knew happened just minutes ago. "How do we get out of this one?" The thunder of hooves drowned out the hypocrisy of his words.

"I don't go for this we shit," Jimmy replied, looking around the small station. With a horde of beasts at the front door, there might only be one option.

The back half of the steel and brick building led straight to the tracks. Leaning into the glass, he scoured the area for something, anything, that would change their luck. No cars were parked beyond the rails. Past that, a lot stood about a hundred or so feet.

"I'm not chancing that run," Alberto said. "We don't even know if any of those cars are open."

"Just knock me down and you'll find out," Jimmy replied, the anger unconcealed in his voice.

Alberto shook his head. "I didn't kill her!"

"Close enough." Not the time for the argument. The man would take him out if he had the opportunity. He didn't doubt that notion at all. He knew the other man realized it as well.

"We need to work together to get out of here. There's got to be a way."

"How widespread do you think this outbreak is?" He walked over to the massive display above the door.

"Does it matter?" Alberto's eyes twitched. The man was on edge. What would he do, knowing Jimmy called him out on the murder? Neither could afford to let it go.

"If you want to save your ass, you bet it does. According to the schedule, a cargo train is set to roll through here in two hours. We could hitch a ride, hopefully riding to a place where the virus hasn't hit yet. Or at least to a more fortified area."

The man's eyes flared. "Good idea. I think. Wait. Would a train stop for us?"

"Hell no," Jimmy replied, "but they're required to slow down coming through every station. We can pray the engineer hasn't heard about the pigs. Or if he has, he'll be safe and slow down just enough."

"I ain't praying. God's taken a vacation on this one."

"At least we agree on one thing," Jimmy said. "The freight trains roll slow enough for us to have a shot at hopping on. Most of them don't use all the cars. All we need is one to be open."

Alberto stared at him. Was he already planning how to kill him if they did make it aboard?

"Love the plan."

"Until then, we wait–and hope the doors hold."

FOR THE FIRST FEW minutes, both men scoured the station for weapons and anything they could use to defend themselves.

Jimmy realized that he might need to protect himself against a human, too. It chilled him.

He rummaged through the back office where the ticketing agent would normally be. Where'd they go? He hoped they made it home without one of the freaks wearing his insides on its tusks.

In all the cabinets and drawers, he only found one tool that could be used. He pocketed it, wondering if it could take down the pigs.

"You get a gun?" Alberto asked him, a cautious tone to his voice. In one hand, he held an ax. "I found this next to the fire extinguisher. It'll do more damage, I think."

Fuck, Jimmy thought. There goes the fair fight.

"No," he replied. "Not even a Taser. I guess with everything online now, security's not a big concern. Until now."

The other nodded and lowered himself down against the wall. "Until now."

NEITHER MAN UTTERED ANOTHER word for the next hour. Alberto cradled the ax as his arm flexed with tension. Jimmy's mind scrambled to figure out a way to stay alive. With everyone in his life gone, would it even matter?

Both stared out at the tracks, hoping. The sound of pig thunder faded, with neither of them signaling a meal would be coming soon.

It would be the final quiet moment for either of them.

THE RUMBLE OF THE train shook both men out of their vigilant watch. They stood and shook off pins and needles in their legs. The massive engine car rolled by, at least fifteen feet high. A frightened older man looked through his open window as the air brakes squealed and howled.

Both men ran, looking for an open car.

"Nothing's open!"

Jimmy heard the fear in Alberto's voice as they both anticipated the inevitable.

"The engine," he called back to the man carrying the ax. "Run faster. He'll let us in." God, he hoped so. As they ran past the edge of the station, the storm tunnel of heavy metal decibels opened up and dissipated, leaving only the rumbling and squealing of the wheels on thousands of tons of sheer steel on steel filling his ears.

Five seconds rolled by before the sound of hell arrived.

The horde of zombie pigs arrived. They must have smelled the men as they exited the safety of the station. One by one, they began a cacophony of screams, howls, and guttural grunts. The thrumming of the hooves on concrete created a disjointed rhythm, with some running on two legs, while the fully evolved raged on all four.

How fast could they run?

Ten feet away. He could reach the railing and stairs of the engine. The old man leaned out the window and yelled something that the wind swallowed.

Don't turn around, he told himself. Don't. If you trip, you'll be shredded in seconds. If you slow down, Alberto might throw you under the rails.

Churning his legs until muscles burned, Jimmy reached for the grip above him. His sweat-slickened hand wrapped around it, then his other. Pulling himself up, he jumped. One foot landed on the bottom step. The other missed and dragged along the cracked stones below. The misstep nearly pulled him under, but he tightened his arm and chest muscles, squeezing hard, and yanked himself to safety.

The engineer slid open the door and reached for him. Jimmy's eyes met his. A blind trust bonded them as the old man's face tightened in fear, yet held tight as the younger man stepped up to the top of the opening and dropped to the floor.

When he looked back, Alberto ran hard. He also swung the ax behind him as the horde closed the gap. Miraculously, he struck a couple of the ugly bastards, sending splatters of blood against the silver cars. Jimmy couldn't figure how the man kept his balance, but the will to survive rose above all else. Adrenaline could do that. He wouldn't stand a chance against the ax if Alberto decided to end the partnership.

"I'm going to make it!" he hollered, his face breaking into a twisted grin. "Don't leave me here."

It would be simple just to close the door.

The man disappeared in Jimmy's view as Reby and Paula replaced him, their faces taut in agony and horror. First, Paula dropped, then Reby, as Alberto pushed through. Jimmy shook off the vision. How could he save this man after both women died due to sheer selfishness and sadism?

Because he wasn't a monster. Not yet anyway.

He reached down. Alberto's strong hand gripped his and both pulled hard. Jimmy held tight as the other launched himself forward onto the landing of the engine.

Dozens of the monsters trampled each other as they clamored for a piece of the men's flesh. No. Jimmy dove into the cabin of the engine and hit the hard floor. Seconds later, Alberto crawled through. Just then, a bloodthirsty yowl hurt his ears.

One of the pigs latched onto Alberto's leg and yanked. The man shrieked and spun, kicking hard to dislodge the sharp hooves before the sharp tusks and teeth tore his calf off. Jimmy reached into his pocket and retrieved his own weapon. A long screwdriver. Lame, he'd thought when he found it, but still, it had to do.

He swung his arm down with all his strength and it sunk into the pig's arm that held Alberto.

It squealed in pain, letting go, but not falling.

Both men tumbled back into the cabin and scuttled for safety. The steel door stood open. The old man wouldn't be able to shut it before the pig entered. Yet he grabbed hold of a baseball bat and swung at the head, connecting with a sick thump. More screams joined his. Jimmy saw three other beasts behind the man.

There could be no way they could fend off four of the pig zombies. Jimmy imagined how it would feel when they tore his insides from his belly and chewed them as he still screamed.

Alberto jumped up and grabbed hold of the engineer.

"I'm sorry," he said. With both shoulders, he pushed with all his might, sending the old man tumbling down the stairs. The beasts fell with him, screams reverberating through the cabin.

Jimmy reached out in vain to save the engineer. The pigs didn't wait for the man to fall onto the tracks for their feast to begin. Four maws tore into the thrashing old man as blood and fluids splattered into the air like a macabre sprinkler.

"Fuck." His stomach retched as he dropped to the floor.

Alberto killed another person. All to save his own ass.

He pushed himself against the controls. "I saved you! I did. You saw that, right? He was about to let them into the train. We'd all be dead if I didn't do that."

A hot stew of emotion stormed through Jimmy's mind. Anger. Fear. Rage. Confusion.

Resignation.

The other man was going to kill him. Maybe not then, but soon. The moment his own safety was threatened, it would happen. The ax lay in Alberto's hands. Jimmy held onto the screwdriver. Both glistened in dark blood.

"You killed him."

The other man's face sat in a stony expression. "I saved us. You know it's true."

"But..."

Jimmy noticed Alberto's hands squeeze the ax. "But nothing. We're getting out of here."

Be cool, Jimmy told himself. Stay calm. Stay alive. "Where are we headed?"

Alberto turned his head to look at the control board. Scanning it for a minute, he seemed to relax. "Autopilot."

"That's for planes."

The other grinned. "It's for modern trains, too. Look," he said, gesturing at the array of lights and numbers. "It's all programmed. It'll go right to the next stop."

"What about stopping?"

Alberto shrugged. "Figure it out when that happens. We jumped on. If this thing doesn't stop, we jump off."

"And if those things are waiting at the next station?"

"Then we haul ass and start over again."

The expression on his face told Jimmy it was every man for himself. Alberto would keep him around until those monsters threatened his life. He imagined the pain of that ax slicing into his leg when he tried to run.

"So, we wait."

Jimmy knew only one would survive.

For the next eternity, both men looked at each other, clutching their weapons. Neither spoke. Through the windows, Jimmy watched the landscape roll by. Towns. Cities. Trees. Nothingness. Repeat.

It would end soon.

His mind roiled with what to do when the brakes hit, and the station loomed ahead.

Sometime later, a sign flashed overhead in blue.

Williamsburg. All clear.

Commence arrival.

Alberto stood up and looked out the front window. "Looks clear to me. For now."

Jimmy joined him. Through the buildings ahead, he saw nothing. Nothing but bodies. Cars parked, crashed. In flames. Smoking.

They were here, too. His hand clutched the controls. His other tightened on the screwdriver. Somewhere in the distance, the hog-human abominations called to each other. Did they smell the new arrivals?

"What now?" Alberto looked through Jimmy.

Jimmy knew but glanced around the cabin. Papers scattered everywhere.

"A map," he said, his voice unconvinced of its use. Holding it up, his hand wavered. Colored cartoonish images of historic houses and more spread out across the unfolded paper.

"Does it show any tall buildings? Apartments? Somewhere to hole up?"

The scale was all off on the map. The universe continued to play jokes. "I don't know."

"There's got to be someplace. Someplace with other people like us."

Like us? Jimmy hoped it wasn't so.

The screech of brakes interrupted.

"I guess we'll have to wing it. Teammates?" The smile creeped Jimmy out.

Alberto wouldn't allow both of them to make it to safety. Not with Jimmy being the faster runner.

A shadow crossed Jimmy's soul. He didn't foresee the end coming like this.

The train began its approach, decreasing its speed. The overhead monitor said .5 miles to the depot.

Both looked out the front window. More destruction lay ahead.

Howls filled the gaps in his thoughts.

When they connected eyes, the world erupted much faster than Jimmy anticipated.

Pain and blinding light hit everywhere as the men tumbled into each other.

Alberto swung the ax down as he fell into Jimmy. The younger man thrust his shoulder into the bigger man's belly. It knocked the air out of Alberto, but the man outweighed him by at least fifty pounds, leaving Jimmy trapped underneath. He reached for the screwdriver, but it tumbled from his sweat slicked fingers and hit the metal floor. Jimmy swung a fist into Alberto's balls, dropping both men in a heap.

The ax clanked against the floor, too, but instead of reaching for it, Alberto wrapped his hands around Jimmy's neck. And squeezed. Jimmy attempted to suck in a deep breath, but his windpipe shut in the other's grip. Fear shot out in cold jolts through his veins as he scrambled to escape. In moments, his vision swam.

Alberto closed his eyes, as if shutting out his terrible deeds. Jimmy reached back behind him, realizing the other was too strong to dislodge. He felt for a tool, a weapon, anything, to hit him with–nothing. He kicked out both feet, managing to slide his body over a foot or so. Lights flickered behind his eyes as sucked in a breath that Alberto's hands choked off. Jimmy knew he was going to die if he didn't do something. His left hand reached around and found something. The screwdriver. His weakening hand closed around it and attempted to strike the other in the face, stomach, anywhere. Yet the blackness grew, and his vision swam, drowning.

One chance, Jimmy thought. One shot, if his muscles would cooperate.

"I'm sorry," Alberto said, the words heavy, sinking into Jimmy's ears.

"Yeah," Jimmy replied, his voice soundless without air. "Me too." He felt his knee jerking upwards and then Alberto's full weight dropping onto him.

Someone screamed. Something sharp dug into his chest. The darkness swallowed Jimmy whole as his thoughts faded away.

THERE IT WAS. A tear threatened to fall.

A hotel. A massive one.

Find your way inside. A place this big. There has to be food inside. Safety. Maybe people.

He ran straight into the automatic doors – which didn't open. Chains locked them both inside and out. He pressed his face against the glass. Someone had stacked furniture against the internal doors, from floor to ceiling.

Bastards.

The smell hit him next. His gut wretched as he took in the scene. Bodies lay strewn about the entrance. If he didn't notice a sneaker or boot here or there, he might not have realized they had once been people.

The pigs had shredded them. What had once been men and women hung from the black awning and throughout the high hedges. It reminded him of a madman's Christmas celebration.

He scanned the entrance. There was always a way in.

Struggling not to slip in the mess on the sidewalk, he grabbed hold of a stand. When he looked down, he shook his head.

Authorcon writers and readers! Welcome!

Well, shit, he thought, that's a bit anticlimactic. Writers. Always making a big deal when reality scared the shit out of society. He wondered how many survived within.

He tried both side doors. Nothing. Couldn't risk banging. The monsters would be on him in seconds.

Finally, he found a small window. He kicked it out and crawled through.

Yet no bodies were present. No carnage.

Those damn pigs hadn't gotten inside – yet.

VOICES SOUNDED DOWN THE hallway. He sprinted. People. Live people. They had to be close!

A sign hung above a set of double doors. Ballroom. He tried the locks. Nothing. He knocked. "Hey, please open."

The more he banged on the door, the more he felt anger rising. He survived this long, lost nearly everyone, and now he could be saved, but the jackasses inside ignored him.

Something rattled inside. A lock. It turned. He pulled out the stained screwdriver.

When the door swung wide, a man confronted him.

"What the hell?"

"It's for charity," said the man wearing a feather boa and furry bra and panties. "Welcome." A few dollar bills fell from his left cup.

"Do you know what I've gone through to get here?" He rambled on about his travels, his fights with the pigs, his man-to-man combat. Everything.

Behind the feathery man, he noticed dozens and dozens of people – sitting, relaxing, dancing, writing on their laptops. None even noticed him.

"Do you KNOW what I've gone through?" he raged as nobody else greeted him.

"Shh," one writer said, his glasses askew and a Run DMC shirt barely covering his dad belly. "My chapter. It's killing me. My agent is gonna rock my ass!"

A flurry of people gathered around him. “What’s an agent?”

“Is that like a therapist?”

“Shut your damn trap!” The writer tossed his pages to the ground. “She trashed my last book in a review.”

“What’s a review?”

“My mom reviewed my book!”

Something else sounded in his mind. Something broke.

“Hey dude,” said the writer with cropped hair, “your arm. Something bite you?”

The images flooded before his blurry eyes. His mom, Bertha, Reby–and Alberto.

The fight on the train. He looked down at his forearm. Flesh had been sliced open. The ax. Must have slipped and grazed him before he gutted Alberto.

Nothing bit him. But... both men had pig beast blood on their weapons.

The angry squealing echoed in his brain.

The world blanked out as the screams began. His face grew longer in a hideous mask–the red death spilled around him.

The world became his sty.

About the Authors

MATT WILDASIN

BIO:

Matt Wildasin is the author of THE BACKROOMS, IT CAME FROM THE SEA, BAGGAGE, MELANCHOLIA, THE DEMON IN THE GLASS, EDGE OF TWILIGHT and the HORRORS UNTOLD series (I through V). He lives in Hellam Township in York, Pennsylvania with his family, Vander and Jamie Wildasin.

Q & A:

Q: What was your favorite part of working on an exquisite corpse styled project?
A: I really enjoyed collaborating with all the other talented authors. It felt like a major group effort and made the experience even more enjoyable and memorable versus a standard anthology.

Q: What's a book you'd highly recommend?
A: I know this will probably be the most vanilla answer, but Stephen King's THE STAND is mandatory reading.

Q: What, out of all you've written, is your favorite story so far? Why?
A: I would have to say it's my current WIP. This book is making me delve relentlessly into the dark corners of my life and forcing me to find peace with those trepidations. I hope to share THE VAST with everyone soon.

ROBERT ROYAL POFF

Bio:

Robert Royal Poff is a horror author and poet from Pennsylvania. They've penned a short story collection (CALL TO THE VOID, Definitive Edition), a novella (SLEEPING AMONG WOLVES), and a book of poetry (MORE USEFUL WORDS FOR USELESS PEOPLE). When not writing they can be found taking pictures or exploring other creative visions.

Q & A:

Q: What was your favorite part of working on an exquisite corpse styled project?

A: As the curator and figurehead of the project, my favorite part was learning about all the wonderful authors that agreed to try my scatter-brained idea.

The level of commitment and dedication to the project from everyone involved shocked me and the immense talent on display humbled me.

Q: What's a book you'd highly recommend?

A: My all-time favorite book is JURASSIC PARK by Michael Crichton. Despite being made into one of the biggest movies of all time, I feel the book is often overlooked despite just how fantastic the character writing and suspense is.

Q: What, out of all you've written, is your favorite story so far? Why?

A: My favorite story would have to be SLEEPING AMONG WOLVES as the queer romance aspect meant a lot to me in my own journey of finding and accepting my identity and place within both the queer and writing communities.

NATHAN D. LUDWIG

BIO:

Nathan D. Ludwig is an author, screenwriter, and producer. His published works include LOVE POTION #666, THE COMFY-COZY NIHILIST, and MIDNIGHT MANIACS, Vol. 1. He lives just outside of Richmond, VA with his wife and their two daughters.

Q & A:

Q: What was your favorite part of working on an exquisite corpse styled project?
A: My favorite part about contributing to an exquisite corpse-style novella is the freedom of exploration within your own chapter while still providing narrative structure to the rest of the story. It's the best of both worlds!

Q: What's a book you'd highly recommend?
A: I'd recommend reading JOHANNES CABAL, THE NECROMANCER by Jonathan L. Howard. A fantastic first book in a series of darkly funny horror/fantasy adventures.

Q: What, out of all you've written, is your favorite story so far? Why?
A: My favorite thing I've written so far is my short story collection THE COMFY-COZY NIHILIST: A Handbook of Dark Fiction.
It's my personality to a tee and if you enjoy jet black humor with your horror and dark fiction tales, I think you'll be in hog heaven!

JESSICA EPPLEY

BIO:

Jessica Eppley is an indie author from Wrightsville, PA. Her work consists of fantasy, adventure, horror, and many other genres.
Info on her books can be found at: http://www.jessicaeppley.com/

Q & A:

Q: What was your favorite part of working on an exquisite corpse styled project?
A: Being part of a group project with others for the first time.

Q: What's a book you'd highly recommend?
A: THE INSTITUTE by Stephen King.

Q: What, out of all you've written, is your favorite story so far? Why?
A: THE EXOCTIC BIRDS series, because it took me 15 years to perfect, so I've lived with the characters and stories for a long time!

ROWLAND BERCY, JR.

BIO:

Rowland Bercy Jr. burst onto the writing scene five years ago and has quickly established himself as a talented storyteller. His novella, UNBORTION, was met with both acclaim and controversy, earning him top honors at the 2020 American Fiction Awards and a finalist spot in the 2019 International Book Awards.
Rowland's writing experience has been a rollercoaster ride of excitement and uncertainty, taking him on an adventure unlike any other.

Throughout his journey, he encountered numerous talented authors and many devoted fans who have motivated and supported him every step of the way.

Q & A:

Q: What was your favorite part of working on an exquisite corpse styled project?
A: It was fascinating to witness how each contributor added their unique perspective, seamlessly building upon what came before. It was an exhilarating experience that pushed the boundaries of my imagination and reminded me of the infinite possibilities that exist within storytelling.

Q: What's a book you'd highly recommend?
A: Jeff Strand and James A. Moore's HAUNTED FOREST TOUR is at the top of my list when it comes to favorite books.
The forest is filled with a multitude of creatures, each one more bizarre than the last.
It was impossible to guess what would come next in this strange and terrifying world.

Q: What, out of all you've written, is your favorite story so far? Why?
A: B.I.R.D.S is quickly climbing the ranks as one of my favorite stories that I have penned.
The ending took a surprising turn that even I didn't anticipate while writing it, making the process even more enjoyable for me.

DORIAN J. SINNOTT

BIO:

Dorian J. Sinnott is the author of numerous works of horror and dark fiction. His stories have appeared in publications around the world and have been nominated for the Best of the Net and Eric Hoffer Book Award. His works have been produced into audio dramas on Chilling Tales for Dark Nights and Nightshift Radio, as well as adapted into comics. Dorian currently lives in New York with his two cats. For more info and to read some of his work, visit: http://www.doriansinnott.com/

Q & A:

Q: What was your favorite part of working on an exquisite corpse styled project?

A: My favorite part of working on an exquisite corpse styled project was seeing how each author handled the story and picked up from where the last left off.

It was a lot of fun seeing everyone's different visions and not knowing where the next chapter would take us.

Q: What's a book you'd highly recommend?

A: I highly recommend Eric LaRocca's EVERYTHING THE DARKNESS EATS. I love his grotesque and poetic imagery and it was so immersive in this book.

Q: What, out of all you've written, is your favorite story so far? Why?

A: My favorite story so far that I've written is my short piece "*The Hunger*." It's the only piece I've written that actually gave me a sense of fear while writing it and I loved getting into the narrator's head.

C.I.I. JONES

BIO:

C.I.I. Jones, known in some circles as Caleb Jones, lives in Norfolk, Virginia with his wife, Courtney, daughter, Lorraine, and their hound, Edgar Allen Pup.

His books include A BOY AND HIS DOG, PECKING ORDER, and STEAM HEAT. When he isn't writing he can be found taking care of the feral cats that have overrun his neighborhood.

Q & A:

Q: What was your favorite part of working on an exquisite corpse styled project?
A: It was great to see other writers' approach to storytelling, then taking that and trying to both acclimate to those styles but try to subvert them as well in a fun way.

Q: What's a book you'd highly recommend?
A: I'd highly recommend PALE FIRE by Vladimir Nabokov.

Q: What, out of all you've written, is your favorite story so far? Why?
A: My forthcoming novel, RED HILL PARADISE. This book delves into a lot of personal fears I've experienced as both a husband and father. I left a lot of my own blood on the page for that one.

D.A. LATHAM

BIO:

D.A. Latham is an Army brat, having grown up all over the United States and Germany. When her father retired in 1989, her family moved back to New England. She loves the beach, spending time in her backyard reading and fall. While she mostly reads horror, she loves books of any genre. Writing has always been a passion of hers and she has just recently started to get her works published.
She is co-host of the YouTube show, What's In The Box: Episodes of Horror with Eric Butler, and has been published in several anthologies, as well as having a series of extreme horror shorts, she co-authored on Godless.

Q & A:

Q: What was your favorite part of working on an exquisite corpse styled project?
A: My favorite part of working on this project was being able to combine my writing voice with other authors. We all have different styles, and it was exciting to see us all mesh together.

Q: What's a book you'd highly recommend?
A: A book I'd highly recommend is FUR by Matthew Cash. It's a story about geriatric werewolves that is brutal and heartbreaking.

Q: What, out of all you've written, is your favorite story so far? Why?
A: The story I'm most proud of writing is *Finding Heaven*. I was inspired to write it based on a friend's art and it just took off. It's a dark and erotic look at what we would do to obtain our ultimate pleasure.

MEGAN STOCKTON

BIO:

Megan Stockton is an indie author who lives in Grimsley, Tennessee with her two children and her husband, who is an indie filmmaker. She writes in a variety of genres that all have dark/horror elements, and all of her work is character-driven and immersive. She is known for delivering works that are raw, thought-provoking, brutal, and cinematic.
She has been writing since she was a child and was always obsessed with horror and the macabre. When she isn't writing (or working her day job) she likes to work with the animals on their farm, read, play video games, and watch movies.

Q & A:

Q: What was your favorite part of working on an exquisite corpse styled project?

A: It was so thrilling to be involved with such a talented variety of fellow authors. I also loved the challenge of trying to make the story as seamless as possible.

Q: What's a book you'd highly recommend?
A: My favorite read of 2023 was CUCKOO by M. Ennenbach. It was one of the most amazing pieces of modern literature I've ever read. Truly a once-in-a-lifetime book.

Q: What, out of all you've written, is your favorite story so far? Why?
A: My favorite of my book-children is QUIET, PRETTY THINGS. It isn't my usual, but the characters are so important to me. It's my least read book and I think that's criminal.

STEVE L. CLARK

BIO:
Steve L Clark is an author of horror and dark fiction from Southwest Ohio. Husband, father of three, musician, gamer, and avid horror fan, Steve can usually be found drowning in all the things he doesn't have time to do. Visit the link for updates, links to his work, and blog posts: http://steveclarkbooks.com/

Q & A:
Q: What was your favorite part of working on an exquisite corpse styled project?
A: I enjoyed the challenge of writing a chapter late in the book. It was fun to pick up where nine others left off and try to bring my style but maintain the tone and carry the story forward.

Q: What's a book you'd highly recommend?
A: I love zombie horror, and I have yet to find a book that hit me like SLOWLY WE ROT by Bryan Smith. That book is a masterclass in heartbreak and brutality.

Q: What, out of all you've written, is your favorite story so far? Why?
A: Of my own work, I would recommend my novella, THE DOORS OF CHAMBERLAIN. It's a found footage/haunted house/cosmic mash-up, and easily my most popular work to date.

ANTON CANCRE

BIO:

Anton Cancre's mother wasn't really pregnant with them when she went to see *The Exorcist*, but they tell people that anyway because it sounds cool. They have published the poetry collections, MEANINGLESS CYCLES IN A VICIOUS GLASS PRISON and THIS STORY DOESN'T END THE WAY WE WANT ALL THE TIME, as well as a nonfiction book about *Silent Hill, Nightmares of Blood and Flesh*. They're also a luddite who still has a blogspot website: http://antoncancre.blogspot.com/ . Pronouns: Any/All/Just Not Late For Dinner.

Q & A:

Q: What was your favorite part of working on an exquisite corpse styled project?
A: I really like working off of other people. That whole "Yes, and..." thing. It's so much fun to just take in everything they have done as gospel before making it crazier, meaner, grosser and more intense. I just love that.

Q: What's a book you'd highly recommend?
A: I'm a huge fan of anything Charlee Jacob has written, but DREAD IN THE BEAST is so incredibly heartfelt and entirely fucked up that everyone NEEDS to read it.
Gods, do I miss a world with Charlee still in it.

Q: What, out of all you've written, is your favorite story so far? Why?

A: Honestly, I am most proud of the work I facilitated with other people. There is this great found footage short story I worked with Sarah Hans on that was incredibly fun.

We just need someone to buy it. *hint hint*

CAT VOLEUR

BIO:

Cat Voleur is the author of REVENGE ARC, KILL YOUR DARLINGS, and THE DESERT ISLAND GAME. She co-hosts Slasher Radio and The Nic F'n Woo Cage Cast. In her free time, you can find her training her army of rescued felines and pursuing her passion for fictional languages.

Q & A:

Q: What was your favorite part of working on an exquisite corpse styled project?

A: My favorite part of working on this style of project was getting to meet and collaborate with so many talented writers in the indie horror space.

Q: What's a book you'd highly recommend?

A: I would highly recommend THE DEATH DOULA, by Ali Seay. It's been one of my recent favorites.

Q: What, out of all you've written, is your favorite story so far? Why?

A: I think out of everything I've written, my favorite story might be my debut, REVENGE ARC. That also had a very collaborative element in its presentation, if not in the story itself.

DAVID SIMMS

BIO:

David Simms lives in the Shenandoah Valley after escaping the wilds of New Jersey. His novels FEAR THE REAPER and PIERCE THE VEIL have irritated readers everywhere while his middle grade books keep traumatizing kids everywhere. When not writing, he teaches psychology, counsels teens, plays guitar in a terrible band of writers, and gives ghost tours in a town which holds an awesome mental asylum.

Q & A:

Q: What was your favorite part of working on an exquisite corpse styled project?

A: I loved the anticipation of writing the ending to this awesome project and the pressure of connecting so many dots from a dozen fine authors! It was an honor to have the final chapter

Q: What's a book you'd highly recommend?

A: I book I highly recommend is THE TOMB by F. Paul Wilson as it introduced Repairman Jack, one of the coolest characters in fiction - and a ton of subsequent novels that influenced my writing. For 2024, Gwen Kiste's THE HAUNTING OF VELKWOOD has got to be the best ghost story in the past decade.

Q: What, out of all you've written, is your favorite story so far? Why?

A: My favorite story so far is my novel FEAR THE REAPER as it opened many doors for me and also shed light on one of the darkest chapters in American history that most people don't know happened.

Made in the USA
Middletown, DE
19 March 2024